Y. Blak Moore

AIN'T NO LOVE
A Heartless Chronicle

ALSO BY Y. BLAK MOORE

ADULT NOVELS

In My Brother's Footsteps
Heartless
Diesel Dolls
Triple Take2: Champagne's Kiss
Triple Take
The Apostles
 Slipping

TEEN NOVELS
To Live & Die in Chiraq

First printing: 2020
ISBN 9781734907025
R & M Publications
Chicago, Illinois 60628

Ordering information:
Special discounts are available on quantity purchases
by corporations, associations, educators, and others.
For details contact the publisher.

U.S. trade bookstores and wholesalers: Please contact
R & M Publications
Tel: (312)650-9720 or rhuemoorebooks@gmail.com

Layout/Cover Design by Y Martin Editing at
ymartinediting@gmail.com

DEDICATION

This book is dedicated to
Robert Beck aka Iceberg Slim
&
Donald Goines

BACK IN THE DAY

Pat leaned against her apartment door holding her daughter in her arms. Dee, the baby, was crying and refusing her pacifier. Tears rolled down Pat's face as she slumped to the floor.

BAM! BAM! BAM!

"Stop kicking on my door, Ronnie," *Pat pleaded.* "I ain't letting you in! I told you, go to yo mama house when you get out."

On the other side of the door, Ronnie shouted, "I just wanna see my daughter!"

"Go away," *Pat sobbed.* "Go back where you been. Go finish smoking crack."

"Ain't nobody smoking crack! Yeah, I dump a little coke on my weed, but that ain't nothing; everybody put a little cheese on they broccoli. I ain't gone lie, I been out a couple of days and yeah I got caught up partying, but that was just my people happy about me being at the crib. Plus, I knew you ain't wanna see me."

"G'on Ronnie, I don't want no crackhead."

"Girl, ain't nobody a crackhead! I ain't smokin the pipe, so quit saying that. I just wanna come in and see my baby girl. I don't wanna stay where I'm not wanted. Just let me see my baby girl and I'm gone."

Wiping her tears, Pat stood up as she gently patted her baby on the back to calm her. Dee stopped crying

1

and began to play with her mother's hair as she patted her back.

"Pat," Ronnie said in much gentler tones. "Girl, I was just missing you and the baby. You know I love you! I just want to see you and the baby. That's my baby girl! All I could think about while I was locked up in that stankin county jail was y'all. I knew you was probably gone move on, that you wasn't gone love me no more, but my daughter gone always love me. Y'all the only reason I took probation. I just wanted to get back to y'all."

"I can't tell you was missing us. This wasn't your first stop." Pat said to the door. "I had to hear it from somebody else that not only was you out, but that you was buying crack."

"That wasn't for me, I was buying that for a friend. I really can't believe that my girl is calling me a crackhead. That's crazy! I'm telling you, I'm not a crackhead. I put a little on my weed but that's it. You don't believe me because you haven't seen me. Open the door and look at me and tell me that I'm a crackhead. I'm for real Pat, just open the door and you'll see."

Pat didn't know what to do. She looked around and down at Dee cooing softly in her arms. "You wanna see yo daddy?" she whispered in her baby's ear. "You wanna see yo daddy, Dee?"

Dee giggled and smiled, but Pat couldn't tell if it was because of the mention of her father or gas.

To the door, Pat said, "Look, if I open the door, it's just so Dee can see you. Do you understand?"

"Yeah, yeah," Ronnie answered impatiently. "Come

on open the door. I just wanna see y'all."

Pat thought about it for a moment. "If I open the door you can't come in. You can just see Dee for a few minutes."

"I don't care, I just wanna see y'all," Ronnie replied.

"I ain't playing Ronnie." Pat turned and unlocked the deadbolt lock and removed the chain. She turned the doorknob and pulled the door open.

Wearing a clean white t-shirt, some jeans and a pair of white Air Force Ones, Ronnie looked nothing like the crackhead that she'd been hearing he was. In fact, with his county jail muscles, 360 degree waves in his head and clear fresh from jail skin he was looking rather handsome.

"Hey, little baby," Ronnie grinned as he held out his arms. Dee reached for him and giggled as he grabbed her from Pat's arms and walked past Pat into the apartment.

"I said you couldn't come in," Pat protested without much strength. "You sposed to stay in the hallway."

Ronnie swung his baby around in the air much to her enjoyment. "Pat ain't nobody trying to hear that. I came to see y'all! I ain't gotta stay in no hallway while I visit my favorite girls. That don't even make sense. Ain't that right, Dee Dee? That's right, you know yo mama crazy."

Making his way into the living room, Ronnie took a seat on the couch with Dee on his lap. He looked at Pat. She was still standing in the front with the apartment door open. He patted the couch cushion indicating for her to come take a seat next to him. Pat held her ground for several moments, but finally she sighed with defeat.

Then, she closed and locked the apartment door. She turned and joined her baby's father with her daughter on the couch. For the next hour or so she watched Ronnie play with his daughter until Dee fell asleep.

Pat took Dee to the bedroom they shared and put her in her crib. From the moment she stood up, Ronnie hugged her tightly from behind. He smelled her hair and kissed her on the neck. He turned her around then pulled her close. She wanted to push him away, but it felt so good to be kissed and held after all the lonely nights she'd spent while Ronnie was locked up

"Dag, Pat you shole smell good, baby mama," Ronnie observed.

Pat started to say you do too, but instead, she feebly protested. "Let me go, boy. I don't want you. Go back where you been. I'm sure there's some girls there that'll let you hug them and sniff them."

"Yeah, there might be, but they not you. You my woman," Ronnie murmured as he licked her ear sending shudders through her body. "I still love you, even if you don't love me no more."

His love talk made Pat surrender totally to him as he guided her to the bed. Later, Ronnie was sweating as he got off the bed and pulled on his shorts. He asked, "Baby mama, do you got some squares?"

" In my purse, in the front room," Pat answered.

Ronnie left the bedroom and returned shortly carrying the cigarettes. He took two of them out of the box and lit them both. Ashtray in hand, he returned to the bed, giving Pat a cigarette. For a few moments they were content to lie quietly and smoke their cigarettes.

Y. Blak Moore

Sensing that Pat was relaxed, Ronnie said, "I hate to ask you this, but you know closed mouths don't get fed. Uh, you got a few bucks I can hold?"

Pat shook her head. "I knew it was a catch, you being all sweet and nice. Nall boy, I ain't got no money. All I got is the money to pay Dee babysitter so I can go to work. What you need some money for? To get high?"

Ronnie looked at Pat like she was losing her mind. "Why is you saying that to me? I just got out! What you think I need money for? To get on my feet! Ain't nobody getting high, neither. I'm trying to grab me a piece of coke and get us some money. You keep hollering that I'm gettin high, but I don't get no higher than nobody else. Everybody smoke premos, that ain't nothing. You worried about the wrong thing. Whatever you let me hold I'm gone flip it real quick and give you yo money back."

Pat put her cigarette butt out in the ashtray and pulled the bed sheet over her nakedness. "Ronnie, I ain't even trying to hear that quick flip stuff. You seem to forget I gave you the refund from my taxes last year for your so-called "quick flip" and I ain't get a cent back."

"Damn Pat, I got locked up. How you gone hold that against me?"

" You ain't get locked up right away, Ronnie. If you was really flipping the money, then why you kept coming back getting more money to go to the store, but you ain't never pay me back?"

"Girl, stop playing with me, you know how the game is. Things don't always go the way you plan, but that don't mean you give up. You keep going 'til you come up."

5

"Well, keep going with yo own money because you can't come up with my money, boy."

Pat rolled over onto her side and pulled a pillow under her head, signaling that the conversation was over. Soon, she could be heard breathing regularly as sleep overtook her. Ronnie eased out of bed and dressed quietly. He left the bedroom, and a few minutes later, the apartment.

An hour or so later, from deep in her sleep Pat heard Dee's cries. "Ronnie get up and get her for me this one time, please," Pat whined as she tried to burrow under the covers. "Just this one time, please."

She wanted to go back to sleep, but Dee wouldn't stop crying. Exhausted, Pat reached over to shake Ronnie awake only to realize he wasn't in the bed. She sat up and looked around the room recognizing from the amount of light in the room that several hours had passed. She saw Ronnie's clothes weren't in a pile on the floor where he'd dropped them.

"Ronnie!" she yelled. "Ronnie! Come get Dee for me!"

Cursing to herself she climbed out of bed. She was still naked as she peeked into the living room, still no sign of Ronnie. She saw the apartment door was unlocked so she locked the deadbolt on her door and went to the bathroom to pee.

"Hold on, little baby," she yelled to Dee as she sat on the toilet. "Here mama come! I see yo daddy gone."

After using the bathroom, Pat went to the kitchen and filled one of Dee's bottles with milk from the gallon in the refrigerator. She changed Dee's pamper and gave her the bottle. Once Dee was settled down, Pat headed back to the bathroom to take a shower. In the shower, she soaped herself several times and rinsed off. She was standing under the steamy hot spray of water letting it relax her muscles when a thought hit her.

"I know that crackhead didn't!" Pat yelled as she jumped out the shower. Frantically she slipped her feet into her house-shoes and wrapped her dripping wet form in a bath towel before she bolted to the living room. As she ran into the room she saw her purse was on the floor beside the couch with half the contents on the floor. She grabbed the purse up and anxiously searched for her wallet. It wasn't in the purse, it was on the floor.

"Nnnnooooo!" Pat wailed as she picked up the wallet. Before Ronnie's visit the wallet had contained the money to pay her baby sitter and her light bill, but now it was empty. With the empty wallet in her hand, Pat sank onto the couch. Tears sprang into her eyes.

"I hate a thief!" Pat fumed. "I don't believe this! Ooooouuuuuuu, Ronnie I hate you!"

Sitting on the couch, covered only in her bath towel, Pat cried for nearly half an hour until Dee started howling. She wiped her face with the edge of the towel before she stood up and readjusted her covering. Dee's cries grew louder, so Pat got up and started making her way to the bedroom.

As she leaned over the crib, Dee stopped crying and started smiling. "I hope you don't be no crackhead thief like yo daddy," Pat mumbled as she reached down to pick up her baby.

Chapter 1

"Shay, get yo butt up and get this phone!" Patrice "Pat" Elmer yelled from the doorway of the bedroom Shanice "Shay" Hampton shared with her older sister, Deniese "Dee" Elmer and her sister's daughter, Honey.

"Who is it, Pat?" Shay muttered from beneath the comforter on her twin bed. "What they want?"

"I ain't yo secretary," Pat stated. "Get yo butt up and get this phone!"

Shay threw the covers back off her head and got out of bed, all the while grumbling under her breath. She was wearing one sock, a pair of Calumet high school gym shorts, and a baby doll tee with a peeling, warped Tweety Bird on it. She walked over to her mother.

Her mother was standing in the doorway with a cigarette in one hand and the phone in the other. She was wearing a pair of tight skinny jeans and a bra. Her stomach was smooth except for a horizontal C-section scar right above her panty line with maybe a few extra pounds, but she wore it well. The toenails of her bare feet were painted tangerine-orange as well as her fingernails. Pat blew smoke into Shay's face as she reached for the phone.

"Hurry up on my phone," Pat said. "I've got to call my boo to make sure he got to work on time."

Shay rolled her eyes as she put the phone to her ear.

"Who this?" she asked bluntly.

"This is Trina Freeman," the caller answered. "Is this Shanice Hampton?"

"This her. I don't know no Trina Freeman."

"I'm calling you from the Chicago Board of Health clinic. You had some testing done two weeks ago, correct?"

Shay's mind brushed over her visit to the free clinic to get checked out on the word of a friend. "Yeah, I did."

"Well, Ms. Hampton, your test results are back. We're goin" to need you to come into the clinic so that we may share them with you."

"Why I got to come down there? I'm right here on the phone with you now. Why you can't tell me what you got to tell me now?"

"I'm sorry, Ms. Hampton, but it doesn't work like that. We don't at any time discuss results of a patient's tests over the phone. You're going to have to come to the clinic to get your results."

"Ain't nobody got no money to keep coming over there on no bus. You can just tell me what you got to tell me right now."

"Ms. Hampton, again, I'm sorry, but we can't do that. You have to come into the clinic. If you can get here, I can give you a CTA bus card so that you may get back to your residence. Can I expect you today?"

"Yeah, whatever. Don't think nobody gone be rushing to get down there though. I'll get there when I get there."

"Okay, Ms. Hampton…" Trina Freeman started, but

Shay had already ended the call.

"Pat, I'm off the phone," Shay yelled.

"Well bring me my phone then!" Pat returned. "I brought it to you. The hell..."

Dragging her feet, Shay went to her mother's bedroom door. Pat was stretched out across the bed, smoking a cigarette as she watched television. Shay tossed the telephone onto her mother's bed.

"Pat, I gotta go somewhere, I need some money."

Pat picked up the cell phone. "I ain't got no money for you. I swear, yo ass always want something. You better start getting some money from them boys that be all up in yo face. If he wanna grin he better have some ends. Damn, I thought I taught you better than that. Gone nah, I ain't got no money."

"You got some money," Shay said stubbornly. "I know you got some money."

Pat laughed. "Let me say it a different way, I ain't got no money for you, but I got some money for me. My bae gave me enough money to buy me a new phone and to get me something to wear to his birthday party, and I ain't spending none of that on you. If I need to go somewhere, I call my bae Luther and he come get me in his new Charger. I don't know what you gone do. Tell one of yo little boyfriends to Uber you."

"You frantic, Pat! He still ugly. It don't matter what kind of car he drive, he ugly."

"He might be ugly, but he got my back," Pat retorted. "And as long as he ain't ugly and broke, then I don't care. Who was that on the phone and where you got to go anyway?"

"None of yo business, Pat," Shay said nastily. "You always in somebody business, but you don't never help nobody."

"You better watch yo mouth 'fore I get up from here and smack the taste out yo mouth," Pat warned, though she made no attempt to move. "I'll get up from here and yank the rest of the little bit of hair you got left outta yo damn head. Now get out of my room, bum."

Shay stomped back to her bedroom and slammed the door with such force that it knocked over several items on her dresser. She kicked several stuffed animals out of the way and flung herself onto her bed.

"I hate her!" she seethed into her pillow. "Oooh, I hate her ass! I hope she die! I can't stand, Pat!"

For a while she lay there swimming in anger until she got up and decided to get herself together to go out the door. She had a Ventra bus card with a few rides left on it, but she had hoped to get some money from Pat so she could get some loose squares and something to eat at the restaurant. She already knew without looking there wasn't much of anything to eat in the fridge. Pat rarely went grocery shopping with the food stamps she got each month. She usually got a couple of bags of groceries and maybe a meat pack from the neighborhood store, and the rest of her stamps she would sell so she could have some money in her pocket. Shay knew that if she could count on there being nothing else in the house to eat, there were some Ramen noodles. There were times she thought she would turn into a noodle.

She stood in the mirror and looked at her hair. It was sticking up in all directions. "I can't wait to get me some money, so I can get me a fresh sew-in or some goddess braids," she said aloud as she brushed her ponytail up into a tight fan on top of her head and used brown gel to slick down the errant hairs. She tied her scarf on her head and went to her closet to find something to wear. She found a pair of ripped acid-washed jeans and a Nike t-shirt. She slipped out of her gym shorts and shimmied into the tight, low-riding pants. She picked up a bra off the floor and put it on. Before putting on her shirt, she sprayed several shots of body mist over her torso. As Shay was pulling on her pair of Air Jordans, she heard her mother get out of the bed and walk down the short hallway to stand at her door.

"Where is you going, Shay?" Pat asked, blowing cigarette smoke.

"Why?" Shay asked.

"Little girl, you better stop playing with me. You better be taking yo butt to school and I ain't playing. That man called from yo school and said that you ain't been there in two days, even the twins go to school."

Shay stood up and looked in the mirror. "They don't teach you nothing at that school no way. All they do is preach about what a great future you can have, but they ain't teaching sh… I mean nothing. And the only reason the twins go to school is so they can gangbang, shoot dice and get high."

"You better watch yo mouth, Shay. I ain't one of yo lil friends. I see you ain't gone be satisfied 'til I slap you silly. You best believe that. I don't care if they ain't got y'all doing nothing but going to recess and eating lunch everyday all day, you better take yo butt to school! Keep on playing, you gone be just like yo crackhead daddy. You better take yo butt to school."

"I said, I'ma go, but I got a appointment that I got to be at first."

"I done told you," Pat warned over her shoulder as she walked away. "I ain't got time for this. I'm bout to miss Judge Mathis messing with you. If you get into trouble, don't darken my doorstep and I mean that."

Mumbling under her breath, Shay went to the kitchen to look for something to eat. There was a half a carton of shrimp fried rice in the fridge that looked promising. She knew it was her mother's rice, but she took it anyway. She shoved it into the microwave to heat while she dug in a kitchen drawer for a plastic spoon. There wasn't one, so she took a regular household spoon. Once she was through eating, she'd either put the spoon in her pocket or throw it away like she'd done many times before.

Carton of rice in hand, Shay was about to leave the apartment, when she remembered to get her cell phone off the charger in her room. She could hear Pat in her room, giggling and acting girl-like on the telephone with her new man. Hearing it made her stomach churn as she walked by with her phone. She was unlocking the various chains and locks on the apartment's door when Pat called her.

"Shay, I ain't playing with you. You better take yo trifling butt to school, heifer!"

"Okay, Pat," Shay said, before she slammed the apartment door behind her. She knew it drove Pat nuts when she slammed the apartment door, so she ran and jumped down the flights of stairs to the first floor and raced out of the apartment building. A block later, she took a seat on the bus stop bench beside an old lady and opened her Chinese food carton. The rice wasn't as warm as she would have liked, but it would have to do. When she was through with the rice, she stuck the spoon in her back pocket. She stepped off the curb into the street so she could see farther, but the bus was nowhere in sight.

Several other people had joined her and the old lady at the bus stop. One was a heavyset man. He tried to squeeze between her and the lady on the bus stop bench. Shay rolled her eyes and sucked her teeth as she moved as far away from him as possible. A young boy with a book bag on his back walked over and leaned against the bus stop sign. He had earphones in his ears and was brushing his already wavy hair.

The bus arrived and Shay got on it before every one, even the elderly woman. She touched her bus card to the fare machine, it accepted the fare and she took a window seat near the back of the bus. Shay stayed on that bus for twenty minutes before getting off to catch her next bus. Thirty minutes later she got off the second bus two blocks away from the clinic and started her short walk to the Board of Health facility. As she walked, an old car with huge rust spots blowing white smoke from its exhaust pulled alongside her.

"Aye, baby," the driver called out. "Where yo thick

self going? Want a ride?"

"Nall, R. Kelly, I don't want no ride from you," Shay said with a wrinkled nose. "You look like a sex trafficker. You better gone before I start hollering, raperman."

That was all it took for the driver to get the hint. As he screeched off, he yelled something she couldn't quite make out.

Shay held up her middle finger as she continued on. She was used to all the attention men paid to her body. She knew she was attractive and one of the few things that her mother Pat had blessed her with was some pretty, smooth, chocolate skin and a pair of long legs with curvy hips. The fact that she was young didn't seem to deter the male species from approaching her. More than one of Pat's boyfriends had recklessly eyeballed her and one or two of them even openly propositioned her.

When she was 15, Pat's boyfriend at the time, a tow truck driver named Carl, used to corner her whenever he could and accidently bump up against her. She didn't mind too much because even though he wore greasy work clothes all the time, he was still fine and smelled good. She couldn't lie, she actually enjoyed the way that he stared at her so hungrily. She could tell that in his mind he was thinking plenty of thoughts he shouldn't have been thinking about his girlfriend's underage daughter.

One day she was sitting on her bed naked putting on lotion after a shower, when she sensed and then saw him watching her through the crack of her bedroom door. She took her time applying the lotion, making sure she oiled her long legs real good. She could hear his breathing grow heavy and ragged as he boldly pushed the door open an inch wider to get a better view. She thought he was going to rush into the room. He stood at the room door transfixed under her spell until Pat hollered for him. Shay remembered laughing as Carl noticed that he was holding a cup of water he'd been sent to get for Pat.

Carl sighed as she pulled her door closed. He went back to Pat's room shaking his head the whole time. She laughed because she knew she was a younger, prettier version of her mother, and she knew Carl wished he could have her.

Shay remembered after she caught Carl peeking at her she started asking him for money. Like it was his duty, Carl would pull a wad of cash from his pocket and peel her off two or three 20 dollar bills. After that day he was always good to hit up for a few bucks for a gyro cheeseburger or a couple of dollars for her pocket. He probably would have still been with her mother if he didn't get locked up for stealing cars. Pat didn't date men that were in jail, so it was over before he got to the penitentiary good.

As she made it to the corner of the block, Shay heard the thump of music beating from the trunk of someone's car. She turned and looked back up the block and saw the car that was emitting the window-shattering bass. It was a box Chevy with a custom navy blue and tangerine paint job. The car was sitting on some huge orange and blue rims. The driver pulled alongside the curb to make a right hand turn in front of Shay. She stuck her chest out as far as humanly possible and stared at the driver until he made eye contact with her. Quickly his eyes darted over her body and back to her face. Shay waved.

The driver made the turn, but instead of continuing on, he pulled to the curb. He swiveled his head around to check out the scenery and then opened his car door. He got out and came around the back of the car and stood on the sidewalk next to it. He motioned to Shay for her to come over.

Like he had her on a fishing line, Shay went straight to him. She was already taken in by his vehicle, but his clothes and jewelry had her grinning from ear to ear. He was rocking a fresh Nike jogging suit and fresh Jordans. On his wrist was a watch flooded with diamonds; the ankh that hung from the chain on his neck was just as sparkly with diamonds, too.

"Lil mama, what's up?" the guy asked.

"Nothing, what's up with you?"

"Just riding. Just come from getting my car out the shop. They just put some TV's in it for me. What's yo name?"

"Shay."

"Shay. That's smooth. I like that. My name is Patron."

"Patron? Why they call you Patron."

"I guess 'cause I'm light-skinned and because I grew up over on Western by them Mexicans." Patron looked at Shay and could tell without her saying that she still didn't get it. "Patron is a kind of Mexican tequila. That's alright. Where you from, shorty?"

"Off 79th Street, over by Cottage Grove."

"Them boys is wild over there in yo hood," Patron said. "What you doing down this way?"

"I got a appointment over this way. Why you paint yo car orange and blue? You like the Bears like that?"

"Not really. It's more about being from Chiraq. Look at the seats."

Shay bent down and looked in the car at the blue and orange interior, noticing a wad of cash in the custom made console. There were Chicago Bears emblems sewn into the headrest of the front seats and a huge Chicago Bears' "C" logo sewn into the rear seat. While she was bending over, Patron checked out her butt. He smiled and let go of a slight whistle.

"What?" Shay asked as she stood up. "What you grinning at?"

"Nothing. How you like my car?"

"That's hot. I like that. I ain't never seen nothing like that. What you do, driving a car like this?"

"I'm a trapper, I mean a rapper," Patron replied. "You all up in my business. What you do?"

"I don't do much," Shay returned.

Patron laughed. "Shorty, how old is you?"

"Old enough."

"Old enough for what?"

"Old enough for whatever you got planned. And I ain't scared. So, if you scared then go to church, Patron."

"You think you talking real slick don't you, shorty," Patron said. "There ain't never, no day that Patron is scared. You best believe that. Yo phone on?"

"Yeah my phone on," Shay replied with slight indignation. "What you think, I'm out here stunting? I'm a boss. Give me your phone."

Patron had an Iphone and a flip cellular phone on his car seat. He reached into the car and picked up the Iphone and handed it to Shay. She quickly dialed in her telephone number, stored it, and handed it back to Patron.

"Do you need me to put my number in your other phone, too?" Shay asked.

"Nall, that's a trap phone. I mean a work phone. My job phone."

Shay twisted her lips. "Yeah right, your job phone. I got to go take care of something real quick, but hit me up in a while Patron and we can go get into something."

Patron walked around his car and got in it. "I'ma do that. I'ma hit yo line in a coupla hours. What we gone get into, Shay?"

"Whatever you want to get into."

"You smoke or pop, shorty?" Patron asked as he sat in his car.

"Yeah, I do why?" Shay asked

"I keep some loud and X, Xany, and Percs. I got Lean, too."

"I hope yo hitters ain't that like them weak pills they be having over by Damen. Or the ones that have your head hurting the next morning."

Patron laughed. "I don't know what you been taking, but I got hitters, little baby."

"We'll see," Shay said. "Hit me up and we can get it

crackin.'"

"I'ma do that, shorty."

Shay watched as Patron pulled off with the music thumping out of the trunk with a grin. She was still smiling as she made a call on her cell phone.

"Waddup squad. Nall this ain't no Brisha, this Shay. Shay! Shay! How you ain't got my number locked in? Stop playing with me! Don't be calling me yo little eater's names. What? Wake yo dumb self up boy! I might got us a stain lined up. I won't know 'til later for sure, but I'm just giving you the heads up just in case it's good. I'll hit you later. Go yo butt back to sleep."

Chapter 2

In front of the Chicago Board of Health clinic was a man selling hotdogs from a steam tray cart fitted with a multi-colored umbrella. Several people were gathered around his cart purchasing the hotdogs, polishes and potato chips he had to offer. Even though Shay had eaten the half order of Chinese food she'd stolen from the house, the smell of those hotdogs made her wish that she had more in her pocket than a bus card and some lint. The hotdog man was a bald head giant of a man that kept a huge grin plastered on his face as he dispensed hotdogs and greetings to anyone within earshot.

The overly cheerful hotdog vendor made Shay super irritated. Mainly because the delicious smell of the hotdogs and polishes was making her stomach growl and she couldn't even afford a ketchup packet. Her stomach protested mightily as she walked slowly past the stand almost trying to fill her belly on the smell alone. Silently, she promised herself that the next dude she kicked it with was gonna have to take her to one of them Maxwell Street polish stands to get something to eat, no matter what time it was, day or night. She could already see herself ordering two polishes with extra onions, peppers and the coldest bottle of Pepsi, cherry Pepsi if they had it. Hoping no one could hear her stomach, Shay hurried past the hotdog stand.

There were a couple of guys selling socks, washcloths, laundry bags, bootleg CDs and movies, and loose cigarettes in front of the clinic making a lot of noise as they hawked their goods. Shay walked past them all, wishing she had at least fifty cent to buy herself a loose square as she passed the cigarette man. She turned her nose up at the sock man though. She hated cheap socks. They'd tear up when you were trying to put them on. Half the damn time the movies they were selling didn't show good either. The movie man was always talking about this is a screener's copy, which was the best quality bootleg you could buy, but they would look you in the face and lie. You would get all the way home thinking you got a decent ass movie, but when you put the movie on, people would be sneezing in the background and walking past the screen. Either that or the sound would be all messed up with the characters talking and then their lips would move a second or two later.

"Got the hottest music and the latest movies, sexy mama," an especially greasy looking man announced as Shay walked past him.

"I don't care what you got, don't nobody even buy them no more," she said in a nasty tone as she kept walking. "Shut up talking to me."

The man looked like he wanted to say something in return, but he let her pass.

"Hey, pretty baby, you got a quarter?" a crackhead asked, as he seemed to materialize in front of Shay out of thin air.

"Hell nall, and get outta my face. You need to be

locked up, out here begging from kids. Thirst bag!"

Though she pretty much hated everybody, she had a special kind of hatred for crackheads from growing up with and being around them. Her absentee father was one of most notorious crackheads ever and her uncles, his brothers, weren't that far off. Whenever her family got together for any occasion, it wasn't long before they were telling stories of her father and uncles' crackhead adventures. Her entire family agreed that her father wasn't to ever be trusted. Her granny said that Negro would steal the paint off a wall and that was her eldest and favorite son. She said that he would steal the wet offa water. Her father and uncles were always in and out of prison for robbery, burglary, drug or gun possession. That is until her father got booked for robbing several stores on 75th Street. His dumb butt robbed a store he used to work at for a couple of months without a mask, so it was easy for the store owner and employees to identify him.

This time when he stepped in front of the judge his luck ran out. The short, white haired judge sentenced him under the Habitual Offender Act and gave her father 45 years and he had to do 85% of the time before he was eligible for parole. She could easily recall how hurt she was when she found out, it was pretty much over for her daddy. She actually loved her daddy, when she could get him to pay her attention. If it wasn't for the drugs, she knew he would have been the best father, but crack got a hold of him and wouldn't let go. She still got letters from him now and again, and the occasional birthday card.

AIN'T NO LOVE: A HEARTLESS CHRONICLE

She always promised to visit him in the penitentiary, but she'd never actually gone. Secretly, she agreed with Pat for once on the "no jail" policy. By any calculation she would be in her 40s by the next time her father would be free. She couldn't even begin to think about all the important days and dates he would miss out on in her life because he was behind bars.

At first, she was having a hard time accepting that her father was locked up. She blamed it on the system and the white judge that gave her father the time. That is until one day she made the mistake of telling her theory to Pat. Pat all but lost her mind.

"Girl, you really is stupid," Pat sneered as she puffed on her trademark Newport 100 cigarette. "Ain't nobody fault but yo dumb daddy's. How the heck you gone go stick up the place you used to work at with no doggone mask on? I'll tell you, because you dumb as a box of rocks! He would have done better robbing a bank! At least it would have took them a little while longer to catch him, and they wouldn't have gave his dumb self so much time. Look here, little girl, as long as yo slow self walk this Earth, don't you never waste yo time on no Negro behind bars. That's they world and they can keep it."

Pat blew cigarette smoke towards the ceiling. "If you ask me, they is way too comfortable with going to jail. Probably down there sword-fighting and being butt buddies, if you ask me. I ain't got time for that. My man can have another chick, but he can't have 'nother man. Shay don't ever let me hear about you visiting a jail bird, writing them, or sending them a dime to put on they books. If I ever do I'm gone kick yo chest in. If he go to jail, in my opinion, that's where he wanna be and I'm gone leave him there."

Shay rarely listened to Pat or took her too seriously, but for some reason that speech of hers stuck with Shay; if a dude she was dealing with went to jail it was a wrap. She had to admit, he'd done some pretty bogus stuff to her family while he was free. Once he'd stolen the diamond earrings from her ears when she was little. He had looted the house on more than one Christmas. Things like watches, cameras, phones, and TV's never lasted long around her father. He stole food stamps and money from her mother, paychecks and birthday card money. She had to laugh about the time she caught him stealing the TV, and he told her he was taking it to his friend's house so they could watch the game. That was the last time they saw that television.

Now, she hated crackheads or dopefiends with a passion. At times she would go out of her way to antagonize them, especially when she was drunk or had been popping pills. If she was with her crew and a couple of guys she would be exceptionally mean to a drug addict, spitting on them and slapping them. Once she even shook up a cold 24-ounce bottle of Mountain Dew and sprayed a particularly foul-smelling crackhead with it in the middle of winter.

Shay elbowed her way past the few vendors and the several solicitors in the doorway of the clinic. She hated coming to this place, but it was free and they didn't need a parent's consent to see you about sex-related topics. You could get some birth control pills, condoms, or take a H.I.V. test without having to explain to your mother about your sexual habits. The only real problem was there were always plenty of people moving in and about the clinic.

Inside the clinic, Shay headed for the information desk to talk to the young lady sitting behind it and answering the telephone. Shay stood in front of her for several minutes before she finally stopped answering calls and putting people on hold to look at her.

Shay just stood there.

"May I help you?" the receptionist asked pleasantly.

"I'm 'sposed to be here to see Trina Freeman," Shay replied with as much attitude as she could muster.

" Do you have an appointment?" the lady asked stankly, not to be out-attituded by Shay.

"Nall, but she told me to come in today," Shay said while rolling her eyes for good measure.

The receptionist picked up one of the many clipboards stacked on the desk and handed one to Shay. "That she may have did young lady, but I'm sorry that's not considered an appointment. All walk-ins must fill out the forms on the clipboard and return it. You'll be seen in order. Thank you."

Shay rolled her eyes again as she all but snatched the clipboard out of the lady's hand. "Do you know me or something lady because I know I don't know you?"

"I don't know you, little girl. Why would I?"

"Well, then, I don't know why you hating. I already told you she called me. You got me feeling some type of way trying to get me to fill out this form. You is doing way too much."

The receptionist looked like she wanted to leave her seat and get loud, but instead she whispered, "Little girl, you ain't about that life. Gone head and have a seat. I'm not trying to lose my job messing with you. You just like every other little girl that come in here smelling themselves. I don't know you and don't care to know you. But, what you need to know about me is that I'm from the Low End, so that little tough act really don't faze me. Yo' best bet would be to chill out and go have a seat and I'll get you called as soon as I can. Now outside of that, if you feeling froggy, gone head, leap."

Shay was a bit taken aback by the force of the receptionist's words, definitely enough not to test her further.

"Don't think you got me together. It's just too early in morning for me to be capping with you," Shay mumbled under her breath as she walked away from the receptionist's desk with the clipboard in her hand. She headed for the waiting room to take a seat and fill out the forms. As she entered the waiting room, she almost had to hold her nose. There was a smell of funk in the room that was almost criminal and everybody there acted like they didn't smell it. The room was lit up! She took inventory of the room trying to guess who the culprit was that had the place smelling so terrible. There was a group of four boys, one lonely-looking nerdy girl, a middle-aged lady with her teenage daughter, and two bums. The bums were watching television and drinking the free coffee the clinic provided. She knew it was them that had this place smelling like an alley.

After taking care to make sure the chair was clean, Shay took a seat as far away from the coffee-sipping vagabonds as possible. Taking care to breathe through her mouth, she hurriedly filled out the clinic's paperwork. When she was finished she took her paperwork back to the receptionist's desk. She was prepared to roll her eyes the hardest she'd ever rolled them in life, but the receptionist took the clipboard from her without a glance. Shay returned to her seat and pulled out her phone. She connected to the clinic's wi-fi and opened her Facebook page. She alternated between liking and posting pictures on her Instagram and Facebook for the next 40 minutes, until finally her name was called by a short stout woman she assumed was Trina Freeman. Shay left her seat and followed Trina Freeman back to a small, junky office. There were stacks of sex education pamphlets covering every available subject. Shay took a seat across from Mrs. Freeman's desk. Immediately her eyes went to a huge glass bowl of condoms and morning after pills on the corner of the desk. Trina turned her back to Shay to retrieve her file, when she turned back around with the file in her hand, she noticed Shay's eyes on the bowl's contents.

"Get you some," Trina encouraged while she opened her file. "Many as you want."

Shay leaned forward taking several condoms and pills.

"That's all," Trina said. "Girl, you better stock up. If not for you, give them to your friends."

"I guess," Shay said nonchalantly, as she grabbed a handful more of condoms and pills. "What you had wanted to see me about?"

Trina looked up from Shay's file. "Straight to it, huh? Well, I ain't mad at that. The good news is your H.I.V. test was negative, but I recommend that you take another one in a couple of months. The bad news is you've got NGU."

"What is that?" Shay asked with her face balled up. "I ain't never heard of that."

" It stands for nongonococcal urethritis. It has a long scary name but it's really more of an infection of the urethra. It causes some inflammation."

"Nongon who? I mean what I gotta do about that?" Shay asked.

"It's easily treatable," Trina offered with a thin smile. "Antibiotics will knock it right out. Your partner has to get treated too. Do you know who gave it to you?"

In her mind, Shay was thinking, it was probably Creole dirty self. He stay freaking on Big Belly Shelly and them THOTs from his block. I knew I shouldn't have been with him. He caught me bored, horny, and wanting to get high. I wasn't gone even do nothing, but after I popped that X and got to drinking that Henny, it just happened. He ain't even know what he was doing no way and he got the nerve to be inflaming people!?

She looked Mrs. Freeman directly in the eye and lied. "Nope, I don't know who gave it to me. It prolly happened when I was with my cousin out of town. I got drunk and had a one night stand. I definitely won't do that no more"

Trina held Shay's gaze for a few moments as she searched her eyes for signs she was telling the truth. Shay's eyes never wavered.

"Well Shanice, I'm not going to preach to you, but you've got to be careful out here. Things can get real, real fast. Right now you've only got NGU, but believe me it's just as easy to catch Chlamydia, Herpes, H.I.V., Syphilis, or A.I.D.S. Like most people your age you think it can't happen to you, but it can and does every day. I'm telling you..."

"Excuse me," Shay interrupted. "I thought you wasn't going to preach. What I got to do to get rid of this NUG?"

Trina wasn't shocked by Shay's rude behavior, she was actually used to these attitude having, know-it-all, young girls. Shaking her head slightly, she handed Shay a piece of paper with a prescription written on it.

"Take this to the pharmacy of your choosing or you can get the prescription filled here for free. Any more questions?

Shay accepted the prescription as she stood. "Yeah, where the bus cards you said that you was gone give me?"

Trina opened her desk drawer and pulled out several bus cards which she handed to Shay. Without saying "thanks", Shay left Trina's office and headed for the small pharmacy located in the clinic. Twenty minutes later she was on her way out the door with her medicine and instructions on how to take it.

She started walking to the bus stop and as she came

around the corner the bus was at the stop. She took off running for the bus, hollering as she ran and banging on the bus windows, but it still pulled away from the stop without her.

"OMG!" she yelled as she flung herself onto the bus stop bench and took out her cell phone. She pulled up the CTA Bus Tracker on her phone and saw that the next bus wouldn't be along for 18 minutes.

"This some bull!" she exclaimed, as she resigned herself for the wait. "He seen me and gone pull off anyway. He just treated my whole life. I hate bus drivers! They be capping."

As she was sitting there complaining, her eyes caught the smoke trail of a lit cigarette in the gutter; it was nearly whole. Without hesitation she stepped off the curb and scooped it up. There was some old-lady-colored lipstick smudged on the butt, otherwise it was a fresh cigarette. Shay wiped the lipstick off of the filter as best she could, and regained her seat on the bus bench. Like an expert smoker, she filled her lungs with the nicotine laced pleasure of her found treasure.

As she sat and smoked, Shay decided against going to school, rationalizing that it was too late. Really she wanted to get high; high as groceries she thought. She pulled up a number on her contacts and placed a call. It rang several times before her party answered.

"Waddup squad," she said brightly into the phone. "Where y'all at with it? You at the stu? Who down there? He there? I'm finta come through there. Aight I'm on my way bout 30 minutes. What? Girl nall, I ain't got no Backwoods money."

Shay hung up her cell phone and was content to check her social media sites notifications until her bus came.

CHAPTER 3

Nayshawn and Jayshawn Crawford stood in front of the small neighborhood corner store, eating Hot Crunchy Cheese Curls with nacho cheese, ground beef and jalapeno peppers. They both took turns sipping on a fruit punch Super Hero juice to wash down their spicy treat.

Jayshawn finished his bag of snacks and tossed the bag into the gutter. "Nay, we shoulda went to school. It's dry out here."

"On God, it's boring," Nayshawn agreed as he passed the juice to his brother. "School be boring too, though. The only class I got that be lit is woodshop. That white honky let us do whatever we want to do in his class."

"I don't mind most of my classes, I go to sleep in them," Jayshawn admitted, "but I do hate gym, especially swimming. All these lames be trying to dunk you in the water. I had to let one of them goofies know if you dunk me, I'm popping you, that's on Snipes, bro."

The twins locked hands in the Snipes World hand shake.

"Let's go see if somebody on the court," Nayshawn said.

"Boi, I don't shoot ball, I shoot opps," Jayshawn joked.

"That's 'cause you can't shoot ball," Nayshawn returned. "You so garbage, I be ashamed to admit that you my twin."

The twins left the front of the store and started down the street. They were so busy arguing, they never noticed the car following them slowly down the block. The older model, white Buick Park Avenue sedan kept pace with them as they turned the corner onto the side street. When they were in the middle of the block, the sedan sped up and pulled abreast of the twins. The passenger hung out the window and brandished two pistols and pointed them at them.

"Yeah, y'all lacking while it's cracking!" the gunman growled.

The twins were stuck.

The gunman laughed harshly. "Look who we got here, the Bangout Twins and ain't neither one of them got a banger. Get y'all goofy butts in the car."

Sheepishly, but trying to remain defiant the twins both walked over to the car and climbed in the back seat.

"Sup Cabo, sup Sko," Jayshawn said.

Sko the driver responded with a head nod before pulling away from the curb.

"Where y'all was going?" Cabo asked.

"We was on our way to the park," Nayshawn answered.

"Boy, y'all out here lacking," Cabo said. The pistols were on his lap as he started to roll a blunt. "Y'all lucky it was me or y'all woulda been done, done!. Y'all out here walking around lacking like suckers. I don't even know why I'm messing with y'all like that. Matter of fact, Sko drop the Bangout Twins off where they trying to go. We can't be seen with no pootbutts."

"It ain't even like that, bro," Jayshawn said. "We wasn't lacking, I mean we was, but we ain't got no bangers. On Snipes though, we ain't never no suckers."

"We got nothing but love for you, big homie," Nayshawn said, "but I'm gone need you to not keep disrespecting us. We one hunnid all day. Ain't no suckers here, we just need some bangers."

"You know what? Y'all right." Cabo said as he handed them each a gun. "Bangout Twins, there. Now y'all both got bangers."

Cabo finished rolling the blunt and lit it. He took several pulls and tried to hand it to Sko, who declined, so he offered it to the twins. "Here, one of y'all grab this."

Nayshawn took the blunt and took several hits, he passed it to Jayshawn who did the same.

"That's right, young savages, hit it hard," Cabo commanded. "That's Scotty right there! Scotty have you out yo body! Don't get scared now. Y'all savages right? Well here go y'all chance to prove it. Today is Snipes Day. The opps killed my man Snipes two years ago today. Every year we sliding til we catch a body. You young bulls want some action well you here now. Y'all ready?"

" Yeah, we ready," Nayshawn said. He hefted the weapon from his lap and checked the chamber.

"Man watch that gun, boy!" Cabo snapped. "That ain't no toy. What about you, boy?" he asked Jayshawn.

"You ain't said much. You ain't scared is you?"

Jayshawn had been silent, content to grip the pistol as he felt the combination of weed and PCP course through his body. In measured tones, he said, "Hell nall, I ain't scared. We gone make them opps wish they never would have killed the big homie, Snipes. I'm ready to apply pressure."

"Sko, you see this?" Cabo asked, his voice filled with excitement. "That's what I'm talking about! You hear them young bulls back there? Now they talking like they ready to go! Ain't no chilling on the block, no lacking, no getting high in that playground they be in, ain't no walking to the store, ain't no going to see no chick! All that is dead! Go get yo' gun or get up out these streets because we slidin'!"

Looking extremely unconcerned, Sko reached over and turned up the radio. He nosed the Park Avenue onto their enemies' block. They spotted five teenagers, two girls and three boys sitting on the porch of an abandoned house. Jayshawn got ready to fire from the car.

"Don't do that, boy," Cabo warned. "Ain't no drive-bys, we finta do this right. Don't shoot out the window. We gone do this right. Sko, spin the block and pull into the alley behind that crib."

Sko drove up the street, turned the corner and drove into the alley. He drove to the half-destroyed garage behind the abandoned house and parked alongside the ruined structure.

Cabo turned around in the seat to face the twins. "Look, all y'all gotta do is creep right through that gangway, step out and start blasting. Don't hesitate, don't talk to nobody."

"What about them girls right there?" Nayshawn asked. "Should we wait for them to move around?"

Cabo feigned disappointment. "Bro-bro, really? I can't believe you asked me that. I was just beginning to think that y'all was ready."

"We is ready," Jayshawn said trying to assure Cabo as he shot Nayshawn a dirty look. "We more than ready big homie."

"I hope so," said Cabo. "Look, you think we care about some broads? Far as I'm concerned, them chicks is opps, too. If they not, then why they out there with the opps? All that ain't 'bout nothin'. When y'all come up out the gangway, y'all better bang out whoever out there."

Sko popped the locks and the twins got out of the car. They crept through the gangway on the side of the building until they got to the front. Guns ready, they stopped and listened to the voices of the boys and girls on the porch of the abandoned building. Nayshawn held up his hand and counted to three with his fingers. On the count of three, the twins sprang out of the gangway surprising the boys and girls on the porch.

Surprise, shock and fear registered on the group's faces as they noticed the weapons the two strange boys were pointing at them. Without a word the twins started shooting at their intended targets. The first girl, a short, pretty one, fell instantly; the husky, brown-skinned boy standing next to her fell next. The second girl, a taller, cinnamon colored girl, stood in the middle of the gunfire screaming until several rounds struck her and she fell also. The third boy fell over the porch railing and tried to get up and run but he couldn't; he collapsed in the vacant lot next to the building. The last boy took off across the street at the first shot and disappeared through a gangway. Finally, both of their guns roared to a halt. The twins made their escape back through the gangway to the safety of the backseat of the Buick. As soon as their butts touched the seats, Sko put the car in drive, and pulled off a little too fast.

"What's is wrong with you? Slow down boy before you get us pulled over for speeding," Cabo scolded Sko. To the twins he said, "You little jokers better have hit something with all them shots. I see why they call y'all the Bangout Twins the way y'all empty them slammers. Did y'all score?"

Nayshawn said, "We let them have it! All of 'em!"

Jayshawn just grinned, he was breathless with excitement.

"Man, they was so scared when we popped out the gangway," Nayshawn bragged. "They knew they was lacking! No talk, we just got to blowing. Ole girl, the tall goofy broad, she couldn't take it. Them shells had her dancing, but bro laid her down before I could. They is done!"

"Cabo, you got any more of that Scottie?" Jayshawn asked.

"Just a little piece," Cabo said, handing a piece of blunt to Jayshawn. "You can gone kill it. Y'all did good, I'm proud of y'all! When we drop y'all off, I got something for y'all. Y'all gone have to leave them poles though."

Nayshawn leaned forward. "What you say? It sound like you said we gone have to leave these bangers. I know you ain't sending us out here naked after we just took care of business."

"Y'all not finta be walking the streets with them bangers with fresh bodies on them. I'm finta send them outta town and trade for some fresh guns, or at least out of state bodies. I ain't finta leave the Bangout Twins without no heat though. I got a .380 I'm finta give y'all and I'll pull back on y'all later and give y'all something else."

Cabo turned around just in time to see the twins giving one another a doubtful look. He laughed. "I like that. You little dudes don't trust nobody more than y'all trust each other. I'm a man of my word though, I got y'all. Pass them up here, though."

Reluctantly the twins passed the guns to Cabo. They sank back into the seats and were quiet the rest of the drive to the park. When Sko pulled into a parking space across the street from the basketball court in the park, Cabo tossed a baggie on Nayshawn's lap. The baggie contained weed and pills.

"That's a half-ounce of weed and some Zans. I ain't got no more Scottie so that's gone have to do," Cabo said, as he pulled a roll of money from his pocket. He counted out $150 and handed that to Jayshawn. "That's for both of y'all. Buy y'all a drink or something and celebrate Snipes Day." To Sko, he said, "Grab that gun out the trunk and give it to them."

Sko got out of the car and opened the trunk lid. From under the spare tire, he retrieved a .380 semiautomatic. He closed the trunk lid and got back under the steering wheel. He handed the gun to Cabo, who in turn, handed it to Jayshawn.

"That's a good gun," Cabo said. "10 shots in that boy, I got a .357 y'all can have, too. I got to get it from one of my trap houses. Just call me later and I'll make sure y'all get y'all hands on it."

The twins tucked the gun, money and drugs away before getting out of Sko's car. They spotted some of their friends on the basketball court and headed across the street to join them.

CHAPTER 4

Shay knocked and kicked on the basement door that led to the neighborhood studio for several minutes before someone opened the door. She stepped inside the basement and shut and locked the door behind herself. It took a few moments for her eyes to adjust to the dim light as she stepped into the main room of the basement.

Several boys and girls were lounging on the tattered brown leather sectional there. Weed smoke hung heavy in the air and there were several bottles of cheap liquor in attendance. A tall girl with long braids jumped up from the couch and ran over to hug Shay, almost bowling her over.

"Shay! Waddup, bro. Squad up in this mug!"

"What it do, Plena?" Shay responded as she returned her friend's hug. She spoke to her other friends on the couch. "Waddup Cat? Trish?"

Cat, a short, light-skinned girl with big brown eyes and a forehead full of pre-adolescent acne, cracked a lop-sided, but adorable smile. "Waddup Shay? That's my, dawg. On bro nem, I was just asking Trish had she talked to you."

"Why you ain't hit my line, foolie?" Shay asked Trish, putting her arm around Plena's shoulders.

"She ain't have no minutes on that gov-o phone,"

Plena cracked.

"It's worse than that! I ain't got no phone!" Trish replied in between licks of the blunt she was rolling. Trish was pretty with long hair and buck teeth; she was slim and looked to be all knees and elbows. "I'm 'sposed to be on punishment, so my mama took my phone. She ain't pay my bill, but saw I was still getting incoming and using wi-fi, so she took it all together. Aye, you wanna hit this loud, Shay?"

"Girl, don't ask me no stupid question that! Ask do I want pickles on my burger. Ask me do I want to go swimming. Ask me if I want lemon pepper on my chicken, but don't never ask me do I wanna hit the weed!"

They all laughed as Plena and Shay took seats on the couch. Trish passed her the blunt and shortly Shay was puffing up a storm. She passed the blunt and took a sip of gin straight from a bottle sitting on the table by the couch. She fanned herself with her hand as the gin burned its way through her system and deposited itself in her stomach. Instantly, she felt the warming sensation of the gin in her bones. She sat back on the couch and waited for the blunt to make it back around to her.

"You broads just gone smoke up all my weed, hunh?" a voice rasped. It was coming from the little dark hallway that led to the recording booth. A slender, brown-skinned boy with shoulder-length locs pulled into several ponytails ducked a pipe in the ceiling as he stepped into view. He was dressed plainly in a white Polo t-shirt, a pair of tattered blue jeans and crisp white Air Force Ones. The handle of a pistol hung out of his pocket. "I know that's Shay trying to smoke it all up, too."

"Dag boy, stop hating, Ace," Shay said, but there was no animosity in her voice. In fact she couldn't stop herself from grinning. "You smoke up all my weed."

"Yeah, whatever, when you finally have some weed," Ace said lightheartedly as he sat on the arm of the couch next to Shay. He fished a plastic baggie full of weed from his pocket and a pack of blunts.

"Yo' country self still smokin' them Swishers?" Shay asked with a hint of disgust.

"On God, Backwoods make me sick to my stomach. And they be having y'all breath stinking. No, thank you, I'll stick to Swishers and if you don't like it, you ain't gotta hit it."

Shay looked at Ace like she wanted to say he was crazy, but she fell silent and seemed to be content to caress Ace's smooth looking skin with her gaze. Plena noticed her longing stare.

"Dag, Shay!" Plena said loudly as she pounded Shay in the back. "You is really in yo' feelings. I see you looking at Ace like a steak taco."

"Really, Plena? Don't nobody want Ace, I know I don't, I been had that. He in love with his baby mama, anyway."

Laughing lightly, Ace lit his blunt. He inhaled deeply several times before passing it to Shay. He locked eyes with her as she took the weed until she turned away slightly blushing.

"Girl, you would still be mine if I wanted," Ace said

smoothly showing his even white teeth.

Shay couldn't look him in the eye as she said, "Boy gone head on. You too fertile for me! Pat would kill me if I came up in her house with a baby. Plus, trying to fall in love, I ain't even on that, I'm trying to get this money. That's what I love, this paper. Call me heartless because I don't love nothing but this money. I ain't got no heart because hearts get broke and I ain't got time for that. Ain't no love out here."

"Yeah, okay," Trish said after twisting her lips. "She in love. We know that been Ace's every since he took yo' cherry, so you ain't gotta stunt for us."

Shay rolled her eyes at Trish. "I know you ain't talking with yo' super emo, stalking-self."

"You climb one gate and jump out the bushes on one boyfriend and now you considered a stalker," Trish joked.

"Don't nobody wanna hear that," Ace said, exhaling a huge weed cloud. "I'm trying to get high. Y'all keep it up and the guys gone have to ban y'all from the studio."

"Who finta get banned from the stu?" asked a slim boy wearing a sharply tapered, but wildly nappy afro. He came from the studio also. His chipped tooth smile and hairless face made him look innocent, but his deep brown eyes were aged like he'd seen many things in his short life.

The minute Shay saw who asked that question, she could barely mask the dislike on her face.

"It's good, Swan," Ace said. "I was just letting these chicks know ain't nobody wanna hear what they was talking about. Their topics of discussion weren't suitable studio conversation and they need to chill out or get out."

Swan walked over and shook Ace's hand. "That's right my dude. Waddup, Plena? Trish? Shay?"

"Ain't nothing up, raper-man," Shay mumbled.

"What's that?" Swan asked with an amused smile on his face.

Shay looked at Swan like she wanted to say something, but instead she accepted the blunt from Ace. "Don't even worry about it, Swan," she said as she lay back against the couch and hit the weed. As she smoked she thought about the day they were over Swan's house getting high. Some dudes from over by Ashland had hit a liquor store and came through selling fifths of liquor for dirt cheap. Ace and his guys bought quite a few bottles and they ended up at Swan's crib getting drunk.

Shay was sipping Ciroc with some tropical lemonade and before she knew it she was the drunkest she'd ever been in her life; she ended up passing out. The last thing she remembered was them putting her in Swan's bed to let her sleep it off. Much later she awoke and she knew instantly something wasn't right. She had been fully dressed when she passed out, but now her shoes and pants were missing. Her panties were in place but they felt moist. She was still trying to figure out what was going on when Swan walked in the room. He seemed to be grinning even more than usual. He gave her some feeble excuse about him not liking people to get on his bed with street clothes on, so that's why he took her pants off.

There were tears in her eyes as she got dressed that day and went to the bathroom to inspect her privates. She couldn't tell if she'd had sex, but she just didn't feel right. She knew something had happened, but since she couldn't prove anything she had to let it go. Since then, Swan always made slick little cracks about sex around her, but maintained his innocence. That didn't stop her from hating his guts, though.

"Shay, check it out," Ace said in his usual smooth way.

"Wassup, boy? Don't you see I'm chillin'?"

Ace left his seat and started to walk away. "Oh, okay. I thought you had to holler at me. Don't worry about it."

Shay jumped up. "Oh snap, I almost forget. Yeah, let me holler at you."

She followed Ace to one of the several rooms in the huge basement. They stepped into the laundry room and closed the door. Ace lit another blunt.

"What you got for me?" Ace asked blowing weed smoke.

"I told you it ain't ready yet. I just met the dude, but he was trying to flex. He trapping though, talking about he be having pills or whatever. He was stuntin' in a Chicago Bears car."

"What? A Chicago Bears car?"

"Like the football team. The car was blue and orange and had Chicago Bears on it. He act like he getting some dough. I'm saying if you don't know him let's get him. I don't know 'bout you, but I'm broke and it's about to be summer."

Ace blew smoke at the ceiling. "Nall, I don't know nobody with a Chicago Bears car. What was his name? Where he say he from?"

"He said he from over on Western by them Mexicans, his name Patron. He 'sposed to come get me later or something. We 'sposed to go out.

"Nall, I don't know nobody named Patron. You say he got bread, right?"

"It looked like he did. That's what I'm saying. If he come get me like he said, I see what he got on him, if he holdin', y'all pull up when we get situated somewhere, and rob him."

"Simple as that, hunh?" Ace asked as he squinted through the weed smoke. "That's what I'm talking about. These goofies out here ain't ready for Sexy Shay. Ain't no love."

"None at all," Shay agreed.

"Don't let him take you to no trap house, though," Ace instructed her. "If he try to, tell him you uncomfortable. Tell him get a room, unless he a complete idiot and gone take you to his crib. A room is always better. Have him take you to the one we robbed that Arab at on Stony Island."

Shay took the blunt from Ace. "What if he ain't got no bread on him, Ace? I ain't with that torture and kidnapping stuff."

"Girl, do you think somebody ride around in a car painted like the Chicago Bears with no bread on him? He sound like a baller. All lames like him do is flex. He had money, drugs and jewelry on him when you met him, then he gone have paper, drugs and jewelry on with you get up with him."

Shay was playing with the blunt, blowing smoke into the air. She said, "Actually, I was thinking about making him take me to a movie and to get something to eat. Something that you ain't never done."

"Don't start girl. You know my baby mama be on bull."

"Come to think of it. You been acting real shady since you moved in with yo B.M., too."

Ace rolled his eyes. "Gone on with that girl. You know I been busy working on my music. I ain't got time for..."

"Well maybe you ain't got time for this neither," she said thoughtfully. "I think I'll just get my little brothers to do it."

Ace put his arms around her and pulled her close. "Stop playing, Shay. I wasn't saying I'm too busy for you. I was just saying I been busy period. Look, baby girl, I miss you and that body."

"I can't tell," Shay said.

"Well, I can show you better than I can tell you," Ace assured her, taking the blunt from her.

He took a hit and put it out on the washing machine. He helped Shay out of her shirt and she didn't resist. As he helped her out of her jeans, Swan stuck his phone through a crack in the door just wide enough for his phone and began to record them. Ace looked directly into the camera and smiled as he continued to undress her.

••••

In the living room area of the basement studio Shay rejoined her friends while Ace went into the recording section of the studio. Another boy named Fern had joined them. He was playing a video game with Plena sitting on his lap when Shay walked in. Fern was of medium build with a dark chocolate complexion and with white, straight teeth. He wore a short curly Mohawk and his long eyelashes kept the girls in his face.

"Well, if it ain't fine Fern," Shay said as she took a seat.

"What's popping, Sexy Shay?" Fern asked with a wide grin.

"Ain't nothing to life but smoking gas and getting money," she responded.

"Well I can't wait til you start getting some with yo broke butt," Plena commented, which started off a roasting session.

They had gotten tired of roasting by the time Swan and Ace walked back into the room twenty minutes later.

"What y'all talking about?" Ace asked.

"They ain't talking about nothing," Shay said. "We need to be talking about getting something to eat."

"Sounds like a good idea," Swan interjected with his usual devilish grin plastered on his face. "Aye, Shay you got something on your mouth."

Slightly embarrassed Shay make a quick wiping motion on her mouth.

"You got it," Swan said. "Fern, what's popping boy?"

"Nothing to it," Fern answered. "It's dry as hell,

everybody in school. That's why I came down here to see what y'all was doing. I knew somebody was in the stu. If wasn't nobody here, I knew Ace was down here laying down some of that heat he finta put out for the summer."

"You know I'm finta tee up," Ace boasted as he shook hands with Swan. "When my mixtape drop, it's over for these other rappers. Real talk! We finta shoot like four videos too, back to back. Once the shows get to popping we on our way to the money."

"Just make sure when you get to shooting all them videos that I be all up in them," Shay said.

"Don't worry bout that Shay, we got plenty of footage on you," Swan said with a sly grin. He shook hands with Ace.

"What?" Shay asked sharply. "You trying to throw shade?"

"Nall," Swan said quickly. "I'm just saying it's all good. You gone be in the videos. We gone make you famous."

"What's that 'sposed to mean?" Shay asked. "I don't know what you on Swan, you got me feeling some type of way. Stop playing with me, though. You stay slick at the mouth, bro."

Shay stood up and wanted to get to Swan, but Ace grabbed her around the waist. "Girl calm down, he ain't mean nothing. He was just saying that you was gone be in the videos when they come out. You should be happy about that, but here you is ready to start something."

Swan grinned at Shay as he said, "Damn, Shay, get

out yo' feelings. I was just saying we ain't gone front when we get on. Chill."

"Yeah girl, chill." Ace said, as he let go of Shay's waist. "Aye, y'all feel like going to get this food?"

"If you buying, we flying," Plena chimed in.

"Hell yeah, we up," Cat said swinging a set of keys. "We ain't on feet neither. I got my bae car while he in boot camp. His mama heated that he left it with me too."

"Oh snap! We got the whip!" Plena said as she slapped high-fives with Cat.

Shay rolled her eyes at Swan as she held her hand out to Ace for the money to pay for their food. Ace peeled two 20s off the roll of money he extracted from his pocket and handed them to Shay.

"I want gyro fries with everything and a watermelon Arizona," Ace said. "What you want Swan?"

"A steak taco on pita, add cheese and hot peppers," Swan answered. "Mild sauce on my fries and a pink lemonade."

Shay rolled her eyes at Swan again. "I'll try to remember that. We'll be back. Come on y'all."

"I'm straight y'all, I ain't hungry," Trish said. "I don't feel like going."

Plena said, "You ain't slick you just trying to lag behind and smoke up all the weed. I swear you is turning into a hype, Trish. All you do is smoke and pop pills. You so skinny you need to get something to eat."

"We ain't trying to hear that Trish, come on," Shay commanded. "And you gone eat something, even if it ain't nothing but a French fry."

"A fry will fill her little belly up," Plena joked.

Trish didn't say anything as she reluctantly fell in line behind Shay, Plena, and Cat as they filed out of the basement to go get the food.

CHAPTER 5

Deniece "Dee" Elmer looked over at her boyfriend Quincy "Que" Reardon as he sat behind the steering wheel of his Range Rover. He was rolling a blunt with his ever present double Styrofoam cups in his lap. There was a 2-liter of pineapple Crush pop on the seat between them. A pair of Versace sunglasses covered his hazel colored eyes, and the new Bathing Ape hoodie he was wearing didn't cover up a set of fresh scratches on his neck.

Dee adjusted the blazer of her Chanel skirt suit, it was charcoal colored with a ghost grey pinstripe. She had paired it with a salmon colored blouse and a pair of black pumps by Chanel. Her hair was pulled into a serious ponytail and a pair of Chanel eyeglasses rested on her nose.

"So you really gone stick to your story that you got scratched playing basketball?" Dee asked. "Really? You expect me to believe that Card Crackin Que was somewhere getting sweaty shooting hoops?"

Que licked his blunt while answering, "I was playing ball. We was playing for five bands, that's why they was hacking. They was acting like that little bread was worth killing each other over. That's how I got scratched."

Making sure he avoided her eyes, Que poured

himself a cup of lean. He took a sip and lit his blunt. He could feel Dee's eyes on him watching his every move, but he never looked at her.

"Ain't it too early in the morning to be drinking lean?" Dee asked.

"You sound stupid," Que said. "It ain't never too early to feel good."

"I done told you about that stupid word."

"Yeah, aw-ight," Que said as he blew weed smoke in Dee's direction.

She waved her hands at the smoke and started coughing. "Damn boy, you the one that's stupid. Don't be blowing weed smoke on me, I'm about to go in the bank. You want me to go in the bank smelling like weed? You is really falling off messing with them drugs. When I first started working with you, you would have never done nothing like this. Pass me that Febreze."

Que reached over the seat and got the Febreze off the back seat. He tossed it on her lap and offered her the blunt. "You need to hit some weed so you can calm down."

She moved his hand out of her face. "I don't want that. All that do is make me paranoid and sleepy. I already be scared as hell going in them banks when I don't be high. Put that out at least until I get out of the car, damn."

Dee stared at him until he conceded and stubbed the blunt out in the ashtray.

"There, it's out. I can't believe you still scared?" Que scoffed. "Don't my moves always go through? Do you ever have any problems? I know what I'm doing. I didn't just start bussin moves, I was robbing these banks without a gun before any of these finessers knew what was happening."

"I never said you ain't know how to get money," Dee said while spraying her business suit with Febreze. "I know you know how to get to the money, but that be my face on them IDs. I'm the one walking out with them people's paper. Speaking of walking out with they money, we got to make some changes in how we been operating."

"What changes?" Que asked, his face balled up in a scowl.

"I take all the risks so we got to make a few changes. I get the money out, so I know what type of cash you be having. You have 20-30 thousand, you throw me a few bands and keep the rest, next thing I know you're broke. Broke and you don't be having nothing to show for it."

"What you mean I don't be having nothing to show for it!" Que erupted. "We got clothes, jewelry, we living downtown in a dope apartment, my rent cost more than some people's cars. Our daughter Honey don't want or need nothing. We be at all the parties and events. We was in the front row at the Beyonce concert. I can't count how many pairs of red bottoms you got, you got more than me. You got every bag or purse you wanted, you be having thousand dollar hair weaves. New I-phones, huge TVs in every room at the crib, you got yo' own car, a Jaguar at that, and you ain't even 20 yet. What you got on right now? Chanel from head to toe. What else you want?"

"That's all fine and good, but I ain't talking about all that. I'm saying that we should be putting something up, but you blowing money fast. You stay stunting, throwing money in the club, getting old-school cars built. It's time for us to stop playing. We don't know how long this gone last and we need to be putting something away for a rainy day, starting right now, today. I'm not finessing for no more chump change neither. I need at least 60% per stain from this day forth."

"Who you think you talking to?" Que asked furiously. "I showed you how to get this money and now you trying to extort me? You must be losing your damn mind! You lucky you about to go in the bank or I would beat yo' ass!"

Dee took her time pulling out her lip gloss out of her purse. She pulled open the mirror on the sun visor and began applying a fresh coat to her lips. When she was done, she closed the sun visor and put her lip gloss away and took her can of mace out of her purse.

She turned to Que. "Negro, listen to me and listen good. You been in charge and we ain't got no bread. You only one step above these lames in the street, the only difference is you got me. Now if you feeling like you want to put yo' hands on somebody, know this, I'm gone fight back! I know for a fact that you can't fight, and I done already beat yo' ass before and don't blame it on you was high. You gotta know I'm gone mace you, too. Yeah I'm gone coat you, and you better not go to sleep around me ever again in life. Also I'm gone turn my cousin and my little brothers loose on you, and they been wanting a piece of you since that time you slapped me."

The mere mention of her cousin and brothers took some of the wind out of Que's sails.

He started to say something but Dee silenced him with her hand. "You might as well shut up, I don't want to hear it. You been in charge for too long, it's time for some new management. This the way I see it going from here on out. You still set up the moves and I'll buss em, but the payouts is gonna be way different. From now on the split is like this, we each get 40% and 20% of every move we make goes into our investment fund. We not touching that. Our savings, something you seem to know nothing about. How much money do you have saved now?"

"It's hard to save when I gotta pay all these bills and the rent," Que whined. "Plus, I be having to take care of my sons and Honey."

"I don't wanna hear that, half the time you late on the rent and gotta bust a move to get the whole thing. You be more worried about buying your kids every pair of new Foams than to put something away for their future. Little Quincy be wanting five dollar Spiderman shoes and you be buying that boy $200 shoes. And who throws a Prada party for a five year old? That was crazy! And I'm watching all these silly broke chicks participate in that goofiness."

"I already know y'all just be trying to do it for the Gram and the Book and at first I was too, but I'm not on none of that no more. I'm more concerned about what Honey gone have if something happen to us. You act like what we doing legal. If we ever get jammed up, I want her took care of and I think this is the way to do it. I'm working on making sure we got something from this day forth, what you do with your money is on you. You can still stunt in the club, buy all the shoes and clothes you want, but I'll be saving."

"Now if you don't agree, you might as well drop me off at Pat's house because I ain't going in this bank today or any other bank on no day. Before you think I can be replaced, remember what was happening before you started using me. They was robbing you and setting you up. Now what's it going to be? Do we have a deal? Am I going in this bank or what?"

Que looked at her for a very long moment before taking a sip of lean.

"Am I going in this bank or what?" Dee asked. "Let me know."

"Gone head," Que mumbled.

"I couldn't hear you," Dee said.

"I said gone 'head. It's gravy, I'm gone let you take the lead for now. You know this move is you because I can't change the name on it now. My mama was right, she told me ain't no loyalty when it come to this money, that anybody will cross you and that's for real for real."

Dee laughed. "Quincy you is something else. That mama of yours really messed you up. Please don't tell me nothing else she said. Now you questioning my loyalty because I'm trying to do better for our family? Wow!"

Dee pushed the Range Rover's door open and climbed out. She hoisted her purse on her shoulder, shook her head at Que and closed the door. He lit his blunt and took a big gulp of lean as he watched her walk across the parking lot to the bank's entrance. Through the window of the bank, he could see Dee get in the line for business transactions. He finished his blunt and was sipping his lean when Dee came out of the bank. As she came toward the truck, Que climbed over into the passenger seat and waved her around to the driver's seat.

As she got in the Rover under the steering wheel, Que said, "You drive, I'm high."

Dee handed him one of the three bank envelopes she was carrying. "I already split everything up. We saving ten thousand in one day, and we ain't gone touch it unless we locked up or something."

"Locked up?" Que scoffed. "I ain't no dope boy, I don't get locked up. We don't need no bond money, ain't nobody gone get arrested. You need to quit thinking negative."

"Statements like that are why I no longer trust my future and our child's future in your hands, Que. How soon you forget that it ain't been six months since you was locked up in Atlanta for weed. I had to find out the hard way you was broke, especially since big ole Card Cracking Que was just on Instagram making it thunderstorm in Magic City. I had to take a title loan out on my car, borrow from people, pawn jewelry, all just to get you out. Oh yeah, yo mama ain't give me a quarter neither, but she gone say I'm not loyal. All of your homies ain't have nothing on it neither. After that, I said I wasn't gone never have to go through that again. I don't care how much of your money you blow, but we gone be saving and if you want money, you better make money. Now where you trying to go?"

Que filled his cup of ice up with lean. "Take me to the Gucci store first. They got some ski goggles I need. Then take me out west to get me some drugs. I'm going to the club tonight and I want to be fly, high as gas prices and have a pocket full of money to show these haters."

Dee turned the ignition on the truck and put it in gear. "That's what I'm talking about right there. You is too old to be talking about stuntin' on yo' haters. That's so lame to me, but you know what? Do you, if that's what you on, then that's what you on. You want to go to the Gucci store, that's where we going."

"Thank you," Que said as he leaned back and sipped his lean.

CHAPTER 6

The police arrived in full force at the abandoned building and it was now a taped- off crime scene with white sheets covering the three bodies of the slain. A large crowd of neighborhood people and spectators had gathered in the street and sidewalk. There were several people screaming and crying in the crowd. Police vehicles were parked on the street and on the curb with dozens of uniformed officers milling around. Several ambulances were also parked on the street. One body was on the porch, one was on the side of the porch and the third was in the vacant lot next to the abandoned building. On the ground were plenty of numbered cones designating the spent bullet casings.

An unmarked Chicago police vehicle pulled onto the street. The vehicle parked and two CPD detectives got out of it. One detective held the yellow tape up and the other detective ducked under it. The detective holding the tape ducked under and released it. The two men strode over to the officers closest to the bodies. The officers and detectives all shook hands. Detective Farillo stooped down and lifted the sheet off the body he was nearest to, to have a closer look. His partner, Detective Williams, pulled out a cigarette and offered one to his fellow officers before taking one out for himself. He got a light from one of the officers.

Detective Williams, exhaled smoke as he pulled out his pen and pad to take notes. "Who was the first on scene?"

"We got the call first," an officer said. "We were responding to multiple shots fired. We arrived on the scene to a triple homicide. Also, there's one more GSW victim on the way to the hospital. Emergency guys told us the girl is going to make it. These three were unresponsive when we arrived and we radioed for paramedics. Emergency workers pronounced these three DOA, so we called for you guys. Looks like these kids were ditching school about to smoke some weed. We recovered a fairly small amount of marijuana. No weapons were recovered at the scene. Nearest we can tell these kids were all unarmed and there was no retaliatory fire. All of those casings belong to the shooter or shooters."

Detective Williams looked around. "That's a lot of shell casings. Either they had one of these drums we've been seeing a lot of lately or there were multiple shooters."

"I know this could be considered a crazy question but are there any witnesses?" Detective Farillo asked from his squatting position next to the sheet covered body. "Let me rephrase that, are there any witnesses willing to talk to us?"

Another uniformed police officer spoke up. "Well, I don't know how willing he is to talk, but we do have a witness. He was with them when the shooting started and he ran across the street. One of the bodies is his cousin. He wasn't hit and came back when the shooting stopped. He's in our squad car if you want to do a field interview."

"Let's have a look at the cousin," Detective Farillo said as he stood up. "I sure hope to hell he really saw something and wants to cooperate. An unsolved triple homicide in broad daylight of school-aged kids, a couple blocks from an elementary school would look terrible in our jackets, and we've got evaluations coming up."

Detective Williams nodded. "Not to mention what they gonna do to us in the media. It's gonna be a bloodbath for real. I better call the Mrs. and let her know it's gonna be plenty of overtime coming soon. Hope this doesn't interfere with our bowling league night."

Farillo laughed. "I don't know why you don't want to miss bowling. Your team won't mind too much if you did. Officer, show us the way to your unit so we can talk to the kid."

The police officers lead the detectives over to their unit. One officer opened the rear door so the detectives can see the witness. The boy, Anthony, was openly crying. The detectives decided to give him a moment to compose himself. Farillo noticed that he's wearing handcuffs behind his back.

"Officers, is he under arrest?" Farillo asked.

"Not that we know of detective," the first officer answered. "We ran his name, no warrants, no wants in Cook County."

"Hey man, take the bracelets off this kid," Williams

commanded. "That don't even make sense, he's handcuffed and he hasn't done anything."

"I was trying to tell they goofy ass," Anthony said through his tears. "My cuzzo is dead and they got me in handcuffs. This so fu! They ain't never just kilt my cuzzo like that!"

The second police officer, a shorter guy with a big belly, stooped into the car and unlocked the handcuffs. The policeman was clearly unhappy as he returned the cuffs to his belt and stepped back out of the way. Detective Williams leaned against the car and pulled out his pack of cigarettes. He held the pack in the car and Anthony took a cigarette. Williams took a lighter out of his pocket and lit Anthony's cigarette. Anthony leaned his head against the mesh in the back seat and smoked his cigarette.

The fat, angry cop called out, "Detective, he can't smoke in that car. He's got to get out and smoke."
Anthony started to say something, but Farillo cut him off.

"Just step out and smoke," Farillo suggested. "No big deal. I don't let my partner smoke in the car, it's a personal choice."

Anthony wiped the tears from his face with his t-shirt and got out of the car. He leaned against the police cruiser and smoked his cigarette.

Sorry about your cousin, little brother," Williams said. "My condolences, Anthony. It is Anthony, right?"

"Yeah."

"What were you guys doing out here, Anthony?" Farillo asked. "We know you should have been in school."

"We wasn't doing nothing, man. We was on our way to school, on the dead we was just stopping to smoke this little weed. Chicks be all on my cousin because he play football."

"If you don't mind me asking, was he any good?" Detective Williams inquired.

Anthony's tears started to fall again. He said proudly, "He was good as hell. He was only a sophomore and colleges was already sweating him, real colleges, too. He was the best running back our school ever seen. He been in the papers like six or seven times since last season. My cuddo was going to the NFL and they killed him."

Farillo moved directly in front of Anthony. "You're saying they, who is they? Did you recognize somebody? Were y'all beefing with somebody?"

Anthony looked at Farillo like he was crazy. "We don't bang. We not with no gang. We chill and cuzzo play ball. We was trying to get out of here, not die here."

"You said they, it was more than one shooter, huh?" Williams asked. "Did y'all know them?"

"Yeah, it was two of them. They came out the gang way and they ain't do no talking. One minute we smoking our little weed, then they stepped out on the side of the porch and they both got big guns. Without saying a word they just started shooting. Wasn't nothing I could do, so I skated, hoping they ain't shoot me in the back. I ran across the street, went through the gangway, and waited 'til they stopped blazing. I peeked out and saw they was gone, so I came back. Everybody was dead. 'Cept for that one chick and she was bleeding bad."

"It just don't make sense," Detective Farillo said. "You sure you didn't step on some guy's shoe at the store or something? That's a lot of bullets for you guys not to have done anything to anyone."

Anthony flicked his cigarette butt into the gutter. "I'm telling you man, we don't get into it man. Every young Black boy don't bang. We play video games,smoke weed and party. Everybody around here knows that."

Williams put his hand on Anthony's shoulder. "Well, obviously somebody doesn't know you weren't with it, because if they did your cousin wouldn't be dead. Look, we gonna have these officers run you to the station. After a sandwich, something to drink and a chance to sit down maybe, just maybe you'll think of something. We'll see you in a bit. Come on, Farillo."

"One sec," Farillo said before he stepped over to the two uniformed officers. "Take him to the station, and no cuffs this time fellas. He won't give you a problem."

The detectives walked over to the body in the vacant lot. Detective Williams lifted the sheet so they can get a look at the dead boy. Several exit wounds were immediately visible and he was lying in a pool of blood.

"So, what you think, Williams? You think Anthony's telling the truth, that they weren't banging?"

"Sounds like he was telling the truth. Usually the bangers are more than happy to claim their set and swear revenge. Since he's going to the station anyway we can have another interview and see if anything's changed, but for the most part I believe him. What's this set anyway?"

Det. Williams looked around the block. He noticed a large set of lettering scrawled on the side of a building across the street, it read WE GLAD U DEAD SNIPES, REST IN PISS. He pointed it out to his partner.

"Whew, that's a pretty strong sentiment," Farillo said.

"Yeah, that is super disrespectful," Detective Williams agreed.

While the homicide detectives were being amazed at the sheer negativity expressed by the graffiti, the crime scene photographer walked up to them.

"I pretty much got everything worth getting, guys," the photographer announced. "Any special requests before I leave?"

"Get me a shot of that," said Det. Williams indicating the graffiti. "Other than that we're good. Farillo follow me, I've got a question for our friend Anthony."

Back at the police car, Williams opened the back door. "Anthony, you mind if I ask you another question?"

Anthony didn't even look up. "I did think of something while I was sitting here. Both of the shooters was about the same height and build too. It was like seeing double almost. It was their eyes, they looked just alike. I only got a glance before I had to get up outta there, but they looked exactly alike unless I was tweaking. The weed we had was deeso, it wasn't no Scottie or nothing, so I know I wasn't hallucinating."

"I know what loud and Reggie is, but I been hearing about Scottie a lot lately," Farillo said. "What's that Anthony?"

"That's dip, the wet. It be having these dudes straight crazy. They be smoking that stuff and straight killing people thinking they in a videogame or something. I stay away from it 'cause it have you out yo' body."

"You're from this neighborhood right?" asked Williams. "What they call this neighborhood?"

"This is Sleezo World"

"Sleezo World?" Farillo repeated.

"Yeah, this dude name Sleezo used to run it around here but he got killed a couple of years ago."

"And who is Snipes?" Williams asked.

"I don't know, but they be saying they smoking on a Snipes pack. I think he had something to do with Sleezo getting killed. Whoever it is, they hate him."

Det. Farillo closed the car door and signaled the officer behind the wheel to pull off.

"I don't want to put the cart before the horse Farillo, but maybe, just maybe Snipes and Sleezo are the reason for our triple. Come on, I gotta use the computer in the car real quick."

Williams and Farillo walked to their car. Inside the car, Williams began to type on the computer. Farillo checked his cell phone to pass time.

"Bingo!" Williams exclaimed, succeeding in startling Farillo. "Here it is, here it is. Jackpot baby! Wesley Smith aka Snipes was killed two years ago to this very day. What makes this very interesting is that he was detained and questioned for the murder of Stanley "Sleezo" Pointer, but released because there wasn't enough evidence to charge him. It is supposed to be all part of some street beef that spiraled out of control."

Det. Farillo started the car and pulled out of the parking space. "Well, that answers that question. We've got a triple homicide in Sleezo World on the anniversary of the day Snipes was murdered. Coincidence?"

"There's no such thing," Williams answered.

CHAPTER 7_

Plena pushed wide the door of the sandwich shop and they all filed in: Cat, Trish, and Shay. There were two girls already in line at the bulletproof window ordering their food. As they got in line behind the two girls, Plena and Shay were both deciding loudly on their food choice. They began arguing about which sandwich had more meat, a gyro or the Italian beef. Their bickering made the girls in front of them turn around and roll their eyes. Too late the two girls recognized they were outnumbered.

Shay grabbed Plena's shoulder. "Plena, look at who we got here."

As Plena stopped looking at the pictures of sandwiches and meals on the restaurant walls, she said, "Well, lookie here! Cat, you see this? Ain't this little miss chair-kicker and her friend?"

"Yeah, that's her," Cat said. "Yeah, that's the chair-kicking chick and her little smack-talking friend."

"Chair-kicker?" Trish asked with a puzzled look on her face.

"Dag, girl, you be too high! You don't even be knowin' what's going on, Trish," Shay said. "This chick kicked the back of Cat's chair the whole time they was on a bus on a college tour, while her little friend Kimmie talked crazy the whole ride about what they was gone do to me. All the time, this goofy broad is trippin' over Ace, like he don't live with his whole baby mama."

Shay, Plena, and Cat all stepped closer to the two girls.

"Now, Cat, what exactly was big-mouth here sayin'?" Shay asked as she put her hand in her pocket.

"The little one was saying ain't finta be no talking when they see Shay. It's on sight when I see Shay, THOT this, and THOT that. Chair-kicking Tierra, though, was talking extra greasy 'bout chicks must don't know her, she a boss, and all this other Tough Tony nonsense. When I got off the bus, they was 'spose to jump me, but it just so happened my guy picked me up."

The fear on the two girls' faces was evident. Tierra spoke up, "We ain't even on that. We too cute for all that fighting and drama. We ain't finta be…"

Tierra couldn't finish her sentence because Shay whipped out her pepper spray and sprayed Tierra in her mouth and eyes. While she screamed and rubbed her face and eyes, Shay and Plena proceeded to beat her down. Trish reached out and snatched a thin gold chain with a diamond angel charm off of Kimmie's neck, and then she and Cat started whaling on Kimmie. When they got her down on the ground, Cat plopped down on her chest and started slamming her head on the floor. Trish stopped beating on her and untangled the girl's purse. Quickly she rifled through the purse taking out Kimmie's cell phone and some money. She threw the purse on the ground and joined

Shay and Plena in stomping Tierra. Trish kicked her a couple of times then stooped down and went in her pockets. She extracted a thin wad of bills and a cell phone. She stuffed those in her own pockets.

By now the Arab store owner and his two cooks were coming out of the gated kitchen to break up the fight. They were shouting loudly in a mixture of Arabic, English, and slang.

"Come on y'all!" Shay shouted.

They all bolted out the door and ran two blocks before stopping and resting on the steps of a church.

"What we running for? We whupped them!" Plena said.

They all laughed as they caught their breath. They began to give one another a blow by blow description of each of their participation in the brawl. Trish was decidedly quiet, just nodding and smiling. Finally, Shay stood to her feet.

"Come on, y'all," she said.

"Where we goin'?" Plena asked.

"To get the food," Shay stated.

"How we gone go back to the store we just stomped them in?" Cat asked. "Plus, we gotta go back and get the car."

"Y'all so dumb, that ain't the only restaurant," Shay said matter-of-factly. "Trish, what you get out that girl's pocket?"

"Nothin'," Trish said with a straight face

"I thought you got a cell phone," Plena said. "I could have sworn you got a cell phone."

"Didn't you snatch a chain off Kimmie?" Cat asked.

"I snatched it and I did have a phone, but I dropped them when them Arabs came running out the back. I got scared. Come on y'all, I'm hungry now."

The other girls looked at Trish and at each other, they shrugged and headed back to get the car and find another restaurant.

CHAPTER 8

Nayshawn and Jayshawn walked up the block to a three-flat building a few streets from where they lived. There they repeatedly rang one of the apartment doorbells.

The building intercom sparked to life. "Who is it? And please explain to me why you is layin' on my bell like you live here?"

Jayshawn leaned forward and spoke into the intercom. "It's the twins, big bro. We came to kick it with you, we know you got that band on yo' leg."

"What y'all got?" the voice asked.

We got some loud and some Xans, bro," Nayshawn said. "Quit playing, Tread. Bust the door down, bro."

"Well, come on up, that's all you had to say in the first place," the voice said as the door buzzer sounded simultaneously. The twins pushed the heavy outer door open and entered the hallway. They took the stairs two at a time to the second floor. On the second floor landing, they took turns tapping and knocking on the apartment door. The door opened and their friend, Treadwell, was standing there wearing basketball shorts, a tank top, a house arrest monitoring bracelet, and house shoes. His full beard and wise eyes made him seem much older than his 25 years.

"Damn, stop playing at my door with y'all ignorant

selves," Treadwell said crossly, but there was no hint of threat in his voice. "Come in and y'all better have some loud, too. What color Xans y'all got?"

Jayshawn said, "Yellow fellows."

"That's what I'm talking about, banana dream high," Treadwell said as he shook hands with each twin as they entered the apartment. Before they could leave the small vestibule, Treadwell nodded at their feet. "Y'all know what to do. Bust them shoes down. You know ain't no walking through the crib with outside shoes. If them feet stank you gotta ride out."

Without ceremony the twins shucked their footwear and followed Treadwell into the living room. They took a seat on the couch and loveseat.

Treadwell seated himself in a large recliner and picked up his Xbox joystick. "What brings the terrible twins to see Treadwell today? Treadwell been on house arrest for close to a month already and I haven't seen neither one of y'all. But when I was out on the block, y'all made sure I saw y'all every day, especially when y'all was smokin' up all my weed."

"It wadn't even like that OG," said Nayshawn. "You know how it is when you in the streets."

Treadwell laughed. "Y'all in the streets now, hunh? Y'all done jumped all the way off the porch?"

"Yup, we want all the smoke, too, on Snipes!" Jayshawn said.

"On Snipes, hunh, it's like that?" Treadwell asked with a smirk. "Did you even know Snipes?"

Nayshawn picked up the other game controller. "Nope, we didn't have to. He was one of the guys and we gone ride for him. That's it, that's all. That's what you 'sposed to do for the guys, you 'sposed to ride, whether they right or wrong."

"That sound good, little homie," Treadwell said. "Man, y'all don't even know the half of it. It's true Snipes was one of the guys, but he wasn't on nothing and he got killed because of some dumb stuff he did. He went out like a sucker trying to hate on somebody from another set over that man's girl. He killed dude and dude's homies killed him. I say it's even, but now because Snipes from the set, y'all acting like he was some kinda saint. If you ask me, he wasn't worth the free rubber his daddy should have been wearing the night he made him. He was a no-money-getting bum that kept up a lot of mess and got a lot of the guys hurt or killed. The world is a better place without him! I, personally, hate Snipes and everything he stood for. I would get drunk and go piss on his grave, but he ain't worth wasting some good liquor."

The twins glared at Treadwell for a long, hard moment for disrespecting Snipes' name before Nayshawn said, "That ain't cool disrespecting the dead like that, fam. That's crazy."

Treadwell never looked away from the video game he was playing. "What? I been telling y'all for awhile leave these gang-banging goofies alone and go to school. Get you some bread or something. Y'all wanna be shooters though, how much do that pay? Y'all need to shut up and roll that weed before y'all get on my nerves. If y'all ain't noticed, only certain dudes ride for Snipes. Most of us didn't even mess with Snipes like that. Enough about that, where them Xans?"

Jayshawn pulled the baggie of weed and pills out of his pocket. He fished the pills out and handed them to Treadwell, he handed the weed and a couple packs of blunts to Nayshawn. Treadwell paused his video game, got up and went to the kitchen. He returned with a two liter of pink lemonade and several cups of ice. He dropped the Xans in the lemonade and shook it vigorously until the Xanax pills were completely dissolved.

Nayshawn broke down a blunt and started rolling the weed, while Treadwell poured them each a cup of the Xans lemonade. He gave each of the twins a cup and took a sip from his own cup.

Jayshawn took a sip from his cup. He nodded his head in approval. "I been meaning to ask," Jayshawn started. "How yo' case lookin', big bro?"

Treadwell had resumed playing his game. "It don't look good, not good at all. They tryin' to choke slam me. I need some bread to grab me a lawyer, but my O.G. ain't got it. I ain't finta blow all the bread I got 'cause if I go down I gotta have something when I get out. I can't depend on the guys. With my background, them people can't wait to do me wrong. If the county wasn't so crowded, I would be booked right now. With the amount of coke and weed they caught me with it would take a miracle to beat this one. If they offer me anything under ten years I'm gone grab it and get up out they face. I ain't finta play with these people."

Proudly, Nayshawn handed a perfectly rolled blunt to Treadwell, and then proceeded to roll another one as he sipped his lemonade. Treadwell lit the blunt and took several hits.

"C'mon twin, grab that joystick," Treadwell said to Jayshawn. "Play me in 2K. Don't get mad and grab your burner when I beat you by 20 or better, though."

"You must already be high," Jayshawn said as he picked up the game controller. "Don't nobody dub me, you confusing me with somebody else, big homie."

"We'll see," Treadwell said as he took a sip from his cup while waiting for the game to load. "We will see my young friend."

As they smoked weed and sipped the Xans lemonade, Treadwell and Nayshawn played several times, but Jayshawn was content to get high and watch while he recited some of their rap lyrics. Nayshawn beat Treadwell in the last game and Treadwell decided it was time to turn the video game system off and watch some television. He was flipping through the channels on the television when a breaking news report caught Nayshawn's attention.

"Jay, look bro!" Nayshawn exclaimed excitedly. "Treadwell turn it up so we can hear it."

A pretty Latino woman was reporting the news live from the murder scene they had created two days earlier. "We're here on the South side at the scene of a triple homicide that happened earlier this week. The victims were all CPS students, two boys and one girl. Because of their age the victims are unidentified, but one of the boys has been identified as a CPS football standout, although he was only a sophomore at the local high school, he was already a nationally ranked player and was being pursued by Division 1 colleges. Another victim, a teenage girl, is in critical, but stable condition at Christ Hospital after suffering several gunshot wounds. She is expected to live. There are no suspects and no one in custody. For more details, tune in to the 5 o'clock news."

Nayshawn rushed over to his twin and heartily shook his hand. "Opps! That's what they get! On bro and nem, this Snipes World!"

Jayshawn looked over at Treadwell who was holding the television remote with a puzzled look on his face. "Chill, Nay. Sit yo' high butt down somewhere."

Nayshawn took a seat, but his face was shiny with excitement. Treadwell had picked up a deck of playing cards and was shuffling them while lost in thought. Suddenly he lost control of the deck sending a shower of cards all over the table, couch and floor.

"Y'all did that?!" Treadwell exclaimed as he jumped to his feet. "You little heartless bastards kilt all them kids?!"

He looked at Jayshawn first, who averted his eyes.

"I don't know what you talkin' 'bout big homie. Did what?" Jayshawn asked innocently.

Treadwell stared at Jayshawn for several long moments. Jayshawn sat still at first, but eventually he began to squirm under Treadwell's intense gaze. To remove himself from Treadwell's scrutiny he began picking up the playing cards. Nayshawn was in his own world, he drained his cup of spiked lemonade and lit another blunt.

"Treadwell, come on, bro, let's play some casino,"

Jayshawn urged.

"Nall!" Treadwell growled. "Y'all shot them damn kids. Nay bring yo ass over here."

Nayshawn left his seat and took the seat across from Treadwell, who looked him in his eyes. Treadwell tried a different tactic, he poured Nayshawn and himself the last of the lemonade.

"My little homie a straight killer," Treadwell said. "Taking care of that business. That's wassup. I knew you was a young bull. You ain't like yo' soft brother, you already out here catching bodies. You a shooter, my little homie? Hold on, hold on, I know my little homie, ain't up in my crib claiming somebody else's homicides? I know you ain't clout chasing like that!" Jayshawn tried to catch Nayshawn's eye, but to no avail.

Much to Jayshawn's chagrin, Nayshawn blurted out, "Those is our bodies! Me and Jay did that! We caught them opps lackin' and took care of our business! We the Bangout Twins, opps bet not get caught lackin' while it's crackin'. We heartless! Ain't no love!"

Treadwell took a few moments to process Nayshawn's confession. He seemed content to smoke the blunt and shake his head for awhile. Finally, he said in an extremely sarcastic tone, "So to show how heartless y'all is, y'all go kill some school kids in Snipes' name?"

Nayshawn shrugged. "If they opps, they got to go. You been in the streets, you know how it go, Treadwell."

"I thought y'all was smarter than that. I keep telling y'all to stay out the way. Y'all told me y'all was gone do the rap thing. What happened to that?"

"We still got bars, OG," Jayshawn promised. "We keeps it a buck though. We rap about what we really be doing. We a hunnid, big bro. You wanna hear our latest song?"

"Yeah, spit something," Treadwell said as he picked up his cell phone to record.

Jayshawn cleared his throat and closed his eyes. He rapped, "Snipe world savages Bangout Twins/you better get ready to die and hope God forgive you for your sins/me and bro kept 60 between us just ask that chick and them opps was on that porch/even that fast goofy tried to run and got torched/heartless no feeling like our hearts got scorched."

Treadwell put the cell phone down, but he didn't stop recording. "You two basically done took them kids lives for nothing? A triple murder? Who y'all was with?"

"Cabo and Sko," Nayshawn said matter factly.

Treadwell shook his head. "Not my homie, Sko. Cabo, I can see him being on that, he love sending shorties off. You know what, it don't even matter. Y'all gotta raise up before y'all have my O.G. crib hot. Don't even come back this way, neither."

"Why you say that?" Jayshawn asked. "How we gone be hot? Don't nobody know we did it."

Treadwell laughed long and loud. "Man, I just don't get you shorties. Y'all don't use y'all brain at all. You have got be crazy, you geniuses done wrote a rap about a triple homi. Ain't no telling what y'all done put on the internet. Y'all just did a triple murder on some kids and you don't think y'all gone be hot? You dumber than I thought little homie. The streets is gone be talking on this one. Ain't no way they can keep a secret. Yeah, Bangout Twins, y'all gotta go. Thanks for the Xans and the loud, but y'all gotta roll."

Treadwell got to his feet and walked over to the front door. He opened it wide and stood there, puffing on the blunt. The twins looked at one another. Jayshawn shrugged. He picked up the weed and put it in his pocket. He drained his cup of lemonade and stood up.

"Let's ride, Nay. I don't know what fam on. Let's slide on the block. Aw-ight, Treadwell."

Nayshawn followed his brother out of the door. "Aw-ight, OG."

"Aw-ight little homies, y'all stay up."

Treadwell closed and locked the door in the twins' wake. He climbed back on his recliner and kicked off his slippers. He was still shaking his head as he picked up the game controller and turned the system back on.

CHAPTER 9_

Dee looked at herself for the thousandth time in the bathroom mirror as she dried off after her bath. She took care to lotion her body from head to heel before she slipped into some lingerie. As she turned and primped in the mirror, she loved the way her lingerie hugged every curve. Her makeup was flawless and her hair was swept up into a curly ponytail. Carefully she sprayed on some perfume. Finally, satisfied with her look, she exited the bathroom connected to the master bedroom.

In the master bedroom, Quincy was lying on the bed watching television. Dee posed at the foot of the bed twirling a set of fur covered handcuffs. Quincy continued to watch television like she wasn't even in the room. She climbed onto the bed and lay next to Que, but he continued to watch television like she wasn't there.

Frustrated Dee sat up. "Baby daddy, what is going on?"

"I don't feel like all that," Que said, without taking his eyes off of the television. He sat up and swung his legs off the bed. He slipped his feet into his house shoes. "Now that you're the boss of the operation, I guess you gone even tell me when to perform my duties in the bedroom, hunh? No thanks, boss."

"Is that what this is about?" Dee asked incredulously. "You're still tripping on me taking over the operation? Boy, in a few weeks we've got more saved than in the whole time since you been scamming. I don't understand the problem. Our system works, why change it? After today we'll have a hundred bands and some change put up and you still tripping?"

"I don't want to talk about it," Que said dismissively. "Money ain't everything."

"I'm gone pretend like you didn't just say that," Dee said as she stood up on the bed. "So, you really mean to tell me that you can see all of this and not want me? Don't I look as good as all them women's pictures you be liking on the Gram and the Book?"

Quincy stood up and turned to look at Dee. He took a long hard look before he shrugged and headed for the bathroom. "Nope. Not even a little bit. Don't remind me of nothin'. Go get dressed, boss, we got business to take care of."

Que went into the bathroom and closed the door behind him, leaving a crestfallen Dee in his wake. With tears in her eyes, she climbed down off the bed and went to get dressed.

CHAPTER 10

Shay and Patron walked through the underground parking garage on Roosevelt Street to his car. The custom paint job on his box Chevy gleamed even in the garage's low lighting. Shay nursed a soft drink from the theater as they headed for the car.

"So, did you like the movie Shay?" Patron asked.

"It was Gucci. The seats was comfortable, but I ain't like them different color nachos and they cost too much. I knew you was a baller when you bought nachos, hot wings, and pops for both of us."

"That makes me a baller, huh?" Patron asked with a laugh.

"Uuhhhh, yeah! You must don't know where we at. The Icon be taxing, that's why we go up on 87th Street."

Patron laughed. "That's the ghetto show. You got to fight yo' way in and out of there. I'm straight. I'd rather pay them little few extra dollars to be comfortable. You ain't really eat nothing in there, you hungry?"

"Yeah, I do want to put something on my stomach, so I don't be so hungry later, but I don't think you want what I want."

Patron grinned. "How you know what I want? What's up, what you got in mind?"

"You ain't gonna go. You got money, you don't eat at the type of places I like. You want to go to steakhouses and all those bougie places. I want some hood food."

"I don't know who you think I am," Patron said as he disarmed the alarm on his car and got in. "I love me some Ruth Chris, Steak 48 and Maestro's, but I still eat in the hood. I got a couple of gyro and super taco spots. Where you tryin' to go?"

Shay opened the passenger side door and took her seat. She turned to Patron. "I really really really want something from the polish stand on 79th and Stony Island. They polishes be fye. I don't know what they do different from the other ones, but theirs be the best!"

Unconsciously Patron licked his lips as he looked at Shay. "Well, where you going after you eat? To the crib?"

"Boy, stop playing, I'm going wherever you want me to go. Plus, you told me you be havin' pills and lean. Was you stuntin'? If you got some X, I would love some. You wadn't lyin' to kick it, was you?"

"Normally I would get offended by someone saying something like that to me, but you don't know no better. Patron don't stunt or lie to kick it. Hand me my back pack off the back seat."

Shay reached over the seat and picked up Patron's MCM backpack. She tried to hand it to him, but he wouldn't take it.

"Nall, look in it."

Shay unzipped the backpack and looked into it. The contents of the expensive book bag consisted of a gun, stacks of cash, several bottles of syrup, a scale, a big Ziploc bag of weed, and baggies of pills.

"Damn!" Shay exclaimed, her voice full of awe. "You had all this on you in the show? I thought you just had on that backpack because it cost so much. What if the police had told you come here and searched yo' bag?"

"I ain't no rookie, shorty, I been doing this. I know if the police tell me to come here, they ain't got no business searching my bag, and if they do I'm gone beat it in court. Without probable cause, that's called an illegal search and seizure. I'll beat it all day."

Shay zipped the bag closed and deposited it on the back seat. "Why you carry so much though? You got everything in that bag."

Patron whipped the heavy Chevy around the underground parking garage corners masterfully as he said, "Ain't nobody got time to be running back and forth to the crib. I keep cash because I might run into a good gamble. I keep work because I wanna be able to fill your order when you call. One stop shop. I'm a trap house wherever I go. I'm trying to ball, not crawl. You feel me?"

"I feel you, Patron you don't be playin."

Patron grinned as he steered the car. "Now, let's get you some food so we can get it crackin."

"Is this gone be all night or a short stay?" Shay asked as she pulled out her phone.

Patron just looked at her.

Shay smiled. "Well, I need to text my sister and let her know I can't take my niece to school in the morning."

"Make it happen, ma."

Shay texted: No room Evything n bag. Polish stand

79th Stony OMW

Ace responded: Bet b ready

Patron asked, "What she say? Everything cool?"

"She big mad, but she gone get over it. We finta get something to eat, then we finta turn up. She just gone have to be mad. I don't care, though. Turn some music on, I'm ready to chill."

"I got you," Patron said as he used the touch screen to turn the radio on. "Just sit back and we'll be at the restaurant in a minute."

Fifteen minutes later, Patron parked his car in the rear parking lot of the Maxwell Street polish stand on 79th and Stony Island. They exited the vehicle and he opened the back door to get his bookbag. As he slung his bag onto his shoulders, a masked figure crept up behind him and slapped him in the face with a gun. Patron dropped his car keys as he fell between his car and the one parked next to his. A second masked gunman relieved him of his backpack and dealt him another blow with his pistol. Shay instinctively melted over to the side to keep watch while her cohorts robbed Patron.

"Turn them pockets out," Ace growled. "Wallet and phones, too."

Using one hand to cover his bloody face, Patron fished his money, wallet, and phones out his pockets and tossed them onto the ground. Swan scooped those items up and stuffed them in the bag too, while Ace stooped down to take a closer look at Patron's jewelry.

"You can keep them lame earrings," Ace said as he held his pistol to Patron's head. "Don't nobody wear plates no mo', but you gotta run that chain and watch. This Rollie better be real, too. And hurry up before I pop you!"

Patron groaned as he removed his jewelry. He said, "That's it. You took everything you wanted just don't hurt my girl, she ain't got nothing."

Swan couldn't help laughing. "You hear this? He actually worried about Shay. I got a feeling she gone be alright, homie. Now pull that belt and we outta here." Patron hesitated, but when Ace moved to strike him with the pistol again, he hurried and unbuckled his belt and pulled it free from his pants hoops. Swan snatched it and put it in the bag, too. Ace picked up Patron's car keys and threw them as far as he could toward South Chicago Street.

"We outta here," Ace announced as he looked around to make sure the coast was clear.

Swan kicked Patron as he walked past him. "Next time, don't front yo' move, goofy. You lucky you made this easy so we don't have to body you."

The trio of robbers ran to Ace's car, climbed in and pulled out of the parking lot. They were all smiles as they drove toward their stomping grounds.

CHAPTER 11

Treadwell poured the boiling Ramen noodles from the pot into a bowl. He added soy sauce and the shrimp he'd sautéed in Teriyaki sauce and butter to the bowl. He placed the pot in the sink, chose a fork from the silverware drawer, and headed for the living room. In the living room, he climbed into the recliner and turned on the television. He was flicking through the channels and slurping the hot noodles when he settled on the First 48 television show. He was totally immersed in the program when during a commercial break, a Crime Stoppers announcement came on. It offered money for any information leading to the arrest of the shooter or shooters in a triple homicide that involved a local high school football star.

Treadwell sat up and watched the commercial with an intense look of interest on his face. The Crime Stopper commercial went off and First 48 resumed, but Treadwell had lost interest in the television show. He thought about it for a few moments and his whole face lit up. He grabbed the phone and it took several attempts, but he finally dialed the correct number to Crime Stoppers from memory.

"Hello, Crime Stoppers. Nall, I don't feel comfortable giving y'all my name, not just yet anyway. Look, I ain't gotta take the stand do I? I mean I don't got to go court, right? I just let y'all know what happened and we good, right? No, this is not a prank call, unless y'all consider a triple murder a prank."

Treadwell listened for a few moments. "Look, lady, all that civic duty and citizen's responsibility stuff sounds real good, but I think I'm gone need to talk to a supervisor on this one. Yeah, I'm absolutely sure you can't help me. Let me holla at your supervisor."

As Treadwell waited for a supervisor on the phone, he finished off his noodles and shrimp and lit a cigarette. He finished the cigarette and was cleaning his fingernails with the torn off corner of a Newport box when a voice finally came on the line.

"Hello. Are you there?"

"Yeah, I'm here. Right now just call me a concerned citizen. Okay, yeah, I understand. This is what I'm saying. I know for a fact who did that triple murder. Yeah the one with the football player. I wasn't a eyewitness, but the killers confessed in front of me. I know that no monies will be disbursed until they convicted. I don't care about that little bread, really, that's the least of my concerns. I'm fighting a case and I want either some leniency or to beat it all the way out. You can't sanction that? Well, let me talk to someone that can. What's the detective's number on the case? Slow down, slow down. I ain't no computer. Hold on, let me get something to write the number on."

Treadwell found a piece of mail and a small pencil and returned to the call. "Alright, go head with the number," he said as he scribbled the number down on a piece of paper. "Alright thanks. Here's a tip too, if you want more people to call in y'all need to be offering more cash. Y'all offering $1200 for three bodies, that's real low my dude, I'm just saying. You ain't gotta listen but I'm telling you, get that bread up and watch the difference, for real for real. All right homie, good looking on the number."

Treadwell ended the call to Crime Stoppers and placed the next call to the detective. It rang for several moments and just when Treadwell thought it was going to go to voicemail, someone picked up.

"Detective Williams? Okay, I ain't ready to give my name yet, but I got information concerning a certain matter of a triple murder. Nall, I ain't trying to get that little reward, I'm trying to get some rhythm on a case I caught and get the suspension lifted on my driver's license. What I get caught with? Some coke and weed. Probation once. I been to boot camp and I been to the joint once for drugs. Yeah, they pretty much got me on this one. They gone try and hurt me on this one, I'm looking at a nine to 45 easy. Yeah, I would rather be at the crib, but I can do the time. That ain't what this is about. This is to kill two birds with one rock. If I can beat this case and get some crazy shorties off the street, it's a win-win. Oh, yeah, I actually got one of them rapping a confession on tape. Yeah, it's two of them. They twins. Ohhhhhhhhh, now you wanna meet? You believe what I'm saying now? I can't meet. It's not that, I ain't scared of them. I got a band on. I'm on house arrest. It's Horace Treadwell. I know you gone look it up, that's the correct address. How long? Yeah, I don't care, I ain't going nowhere. Ok, see you then."

Treadwell hung up the telephone and picked up the remote and started flicking through the channels again. He used the button on the side of his recliner to make the chair recline.

For a moment it crossed his mind that in the hood he would be considered foul for betraying the Bangout Twins, little homies he'd known since they first jumped off the porch, then he thought, They shouldn'tna kilt them kids. Goofies.

CHAPTER 12

Swan dumped the contents of the MCM backpack formerly owned by Patron onto his full size bed. When they saw all the money, drugs, and paraphernalia spread out onto the bed Shay jumped into Ace's arms.

"I told y'all he was holdin'!" Shay exclaimed.

"That's what I'm talking about!" Ace exclaimed. "These dudes on the block be thinking two, three hundred and a cell phone is a stain. Nall, this is a stain right here."

"Y'all better pipe down," Swan warned. "Y'all gone wake up my granny."

"I thought yo' granny don't never come up here," Ace said.

"She don't, but that won't stop her from coming to the bottom of the stairs and hollering up here to see is everything alright. Then she gone be wanting to feed us last night's leftovers and she ain't taking no for an answer. So, we gone have to pause and go eat. I ain't trying to do all that. I'm just trying to split this stain up without all the interruptions."

"What was the leftovers?" Shay asked in a quieter tone as she moved some clothes out of a chair and took a seat.

Swan was straightening out their haul into piles. "Some pot roast, smashed potatoes, and creamed spinach. Don't get me wrong, Granny got skills, she get big in the kitchen. No microwave food neither."

Swan never looked up from what he was doing or he would have seen a look of total longing on Shay's face. She had to wipe the corners of her mouth before she spoke. "Damn bro, I wish my OG would cook. I can't remember the last time she made us some food. She'll cook her and her boyfriend of the month a steak and a baked potato, but that's about it. When she don't sell all the stamps and actually buy some food, it be chicken tenders, burgers and hotdogs. Not none of that real food. I want something with some good gravy and some of that macaroni that come out the oven, not from out no box. Man, Swan, you got me hungry just thinking about those leftovers."

Swan laughed. "After we chop this up, we can go downstairs and get some leftovers, Granny ain't gone trip."

"I ain't trying to hear all that," Ace said impatiently. "What we looking like on the cash, bro?"

"One sec," Swan said. He took a few more minutes to count and separate the money into three piles. "Alright, it was a little over 32 stacks in bread. I gave us, me and Ace, ten apiece and we giving you that 12 and some change for putting us on the move. It's two cuties of weed, y'all can have that. I ain't got nowhere to keep it. Plus, it's pills and three bottles of lean. We each get one."

"Ace picked up Patron's Rolex and slipped it on his wrist. "I want this watch, so just give me some of that weed and some X and I'm decent. Shay you can have my lean, too. Swan you can have that belt and chain."

Swan slipped Patron's chain around his neck. He handed the Iphone and the Glock pistol to Shay. "Dag, Shay, yo' boy even had a pretty pistol. Them baby Glocks be lookin' like toys. Shay be careful with that burner, it ain't got no safety on it. It's fully loaded too, just point and shoot. Even a baby could do it. You can have that bag, too."

Shay picked up the designer book bag and started putting her stuff in it. After they divvied up the drugs, they went downstairs to the kitchen to get something to eat. Swan heaped food on their plates and they took turns putting their plates in the microwave oven. They sat at the kitchen table and ate while they talked about the robbery in hushed tones. When they were through eating, Swan walked them to the door and let Shay and Ace out. He locked the door behind them and went back to clean up the kitchen.

"What you about to do?" Shay asked as they walked to Ace's car.

"Drop you off, then go to the crib."

"You going to the crib, boy? It's early and you goin' home to yo' baby mama? I miss old school Ace. Old school Ace would be tryin' to get a room or somethin'."

Ace popped the locks on his car and got in. "I ain't trying to hear that. Get in if you want a ride to the crib, if not I'm gone."

Shay got in the car. "You can take me by the crib, but I ain't staying. I'm just gone put this up and I'm coming back out and find me something to get into. I'm single and I ain't got no curfew."

"Stay playing with me, Shay," Ace threatened. "I been gone all day, I got to make an appearance at the crib. If I get put out can I come live at Pat's house with you? I didn't think so. Like I said, I gotta go to the crib."

Shay was silent as Ace made the short trip to her apartment. The moment he pulled in front of her building, Shay hopped out of the car and slammed the door. She was halfway up the walk to the front of the building when Ace called her back. She stopped walking and turned around, but she didn't go toward the car.

"Girl, get over here and stop playing with me!" Ace roared.

Like a spoiled toddler, Shay walked back to the car mumbling under her breath the whole way. She leaned on the car door.

"What?" she said with a pout. "What you want, Ace?"

Looking like he was trying to control his temper, in measured tones, Ace said, "Look girl, gone in the crib and chill. We just robbed homie and you don't need to be out here in the streets by yourself. We'll get up tomorrow and go to breakfast anywhere you want to go eat, my treat. Then we can go shopping, hang out, whatever. Just gone in the crib and chill. Okay?"

"Okay," Shay agreed. "You bet not forget to come get me, Ace."

"I'm not," he assured her. "First thing in the morning. Now gone."

Hiding a smile, Shay turned and made her way into

her building. She peeked out the hallway window, but Ace was long gone; he pulled off as soon as she walked away from the car. She fished her apartment key out of her pocket and went inside.

••••

The next day as promised, Ace sent her a text to get ready, that he was about to pick her up to take her to breakfast. Shay got out the bed and started to get herself together.

Pat heard her stirring around and yelled, "Shay, you better be taking yo butt to school! Wake the twins up and tell them get to school too."

On her way to brush her teeth Shay opened the twins' bedroom door and looked in. Nayshawn was standing in front of the dresser wearing his school uniform khakis. He was shirtless as he looked in the mirror and brushed his waves. Jayshawn was sitting on his bed pulling on his gym shoes, a pair of Air Force Ones that had seen better days.

"Pat said go to school y'all," Shay said and was about to close their bedroom door back.

"Shay-Shay," Jayshawn called out. "Shay-Shay."

"What boy? What you want, Jay?"

"Why I got to want something? Why can't I just be trying to see what's up with my favorite big sister?" Shay had to laugh at the puppy dog look on her little brother's face. "Boy, quit tryin' to finesse me. What you want?"

"You got some money, Shay-Shay?" Jayshawn asked, putting on his most humble face.

"I'm broke, baby," Shay quoted in her best Money

Making Mitch impression.

"You ain't never broke," Nayshawn said. "Cut it out, Shay-Shay."

"What y'all want some money for?"

"Duh, because we broke," Jayshawn said his voice dripping with sarcasm.

"Oh, you wanna be smart," Shay said as she started to close their room door.

"Shay-Shay!" Nayshawn said. "He didn't mean that. He trippin'. We ain't got nothin'. Pat still be tryin' to give us dollars like we little kids. She gave us a dollar to split yesterday."

Shay looked at both of their shoes. "Pat need to buy y'all some kicks. Them Ones y'all got on is whupped."

"I know," Nayshawn agreed. "Pat was like since we be messin' up in school, she ain't buying us no shoes or clothes. She say she ain't participating in us being no well-dressed dummies. She lucky she OG, because she be sayin' some slick stuff out her mouth."

"I know, right," Shay agreed. "I just learned to ignore her when she get to talkin' greasy. Hold on, I'll be right back."

Shay went back into her bedroom and pulled a few $100s out of her stash. She returned to her brother's room and gave them $200 apiece.

"Don't ask me for nothing else. I'm gone buy y'all some shoes when I go out later. After that y'all dead."

"Okay, Shay-Shay! Thank you! We love you," Nayshawn said as he snatched on his school uniform shirt. Both of them hugged Shay as they rushed past her out the bedroom.

"We gone, Pat," Jayshawn yelled as they went down the hallway and out the apartment door.

"You two dummies better be goin' to school and you bet' not be late!" Pat yelled, but the twins were long gone by then.

Shaking her head, Shay went and brushed her teeth and finished getting dressed. Ace sent another text: Come down. She grabbed her bag and left her room, closing the door behind her. She hollered, "Pat, I'm gone."

"Go straight to school Shay and I ain't playing," Pat yelled.

"Okay, Pat," she yelled in return seconds before slipping out of the apartment. Outside, as she walked to the car, her face fell when she saw Swan in the front seat and he wasn't thinking about moving. Grumbling, she got in the back seat and slammed the door. Ace never noticed as he passed her a blunt, turned up the radio and drove away. Soon, they were being seated at the House of Pancakes, her favorite breakfast place. Shay's anger at Swan coming along had dissipated and in no time they were laughing, joking and eating pancakes, bacon and eggs. After breakfast, they went shopping downtown on the Magnificent Mile.

By afternoon Shay's bad mood was so distant it was like it never existed. She loved the stares they received as they went from store to store buying clothing, shoes and accessories. They went to the Grand Lux Café for lunch and even though Shay didn't particularly like her pasta, she wasn't complaining too much. In her mind, this day was easily added to her list of Best Days

Ever. She was a little sad when they piled in the car with their bags to head home. Instead of taking her straight home, Ace chose to bend a couple of blocks in the neighborhood as they smoked a few blunts.

As he drove, Ace kept looking in the rearview mirror, suddenly he said, "Oh, hell no!"

Swan sat up, ready to put the blunt out he was smoking. "What, bro? Cops?"

"Nall, bro, worse," Ace said as he pulled over to the curb. "My baby mama."

Shay turned around in the back seat as Ace's baby mama pulled up to the curb behind them like she was the police. She locked eyes with Shay and was getting out of the car with an extra crunchy look on her face. Ace knew the look on her face and prepared to jump out to head her off.

Shay fingered her pepper spray. "Get yo' stalker before I get her clothes dirty, Ace. Don't get her drug out here."

"Shut up, Shay," Ace said as he got out of the car.

As they stood on the sidewalk next to her car, Shay and Swan couldn't make out but every other word, but they knew the couple were having a hearty argument. Ace was restraining her but several times she got away from him and ran to Ace's car. She pounded on the car and shouted, "THOT, get out my man's car!" Ace wrestled her back to her car and spent several moments arguing with her. She sat in the driver's seat and he squatted next to her on the sidewalk in her open car door.

Finally, Ace stood up and stormed back to his car.

He opened Shay's door and announced, "You gotta go. She trippin'. She 'bout to start rammin' my car if you don't get out. Call you a Uber and I'm gone get up with you later. Don't start, Shay! I don't want to hear it, that's my BM, that's where I stay. I can't stay at Pat's house with you and if I did she wouldn't let me see my daughter."

Shocked at how the scene was playing out, Shay climbed out of the car. She waited for Ace to open the trunk lid so she could get her bags. At first, she was so bewildered at seeing Ace so soft that she couldn't even get mad. That is until she noticed his BM had a huge smile on her face at Shay literally being curbed. She grew angry as she realized his baby mama was sitting behind the wheel of a car she'd probably helped buy with the stains she lined up with Ace. She began to look around on the ground for a bottle or brick to throw through the windshield of Ace's baby mama's car, but Ace peeled away from the curb and his child's mother followed behind him.

The best thing Shay could manage was a middle finger salute as the two cars entered traffic. She looked down at her Coach, Adidas, and Gucci shopping bags, filled with expensive merchandise and realized she needed to get off this block with a quickness. Hurriedly she pulled up the Uber app on her phone and ordered a car. She kept her hand on the Glock in her purse until the car pulled up and she piled in with her bags. Her face was extra tight as she thought about how Ace had just played her. She made up her mind right there to never be a sucker for his love again.

The Uber driver tried to engage her in conversation, but she didn't feel like talking so she stuffed her ear buds in her ears, even though she wasn't listening to any music. She closed her eyes and laid back and thought about the best ways to get Ace back for the disloyalty he'd just shown her.

CHAPTER 13

The block where the studio was located had transformed into a huge party. There were plenty of people milling about on the block smoking weed, drinking, laughing and dancing. Loud music pumped from the incredible stereo system of a custom conversion van in the middle of the block. The music caused more than one woman to start twerking in the middle of the street or on the hood of a car.

Plena, Trish and Cat sat on Cat's boyfriend's car watching the festivities. Not more than 20 feet from them, Ace, Swan, and a couple of their homies were passing blunts and displaying their bottles. As they postured and posed their guns were easily noticeable.

A Hyundai Sonata displaying Uber stickers drove onto the block and stopped and Shay exited the vehicle. She walked toward her friends looking like new money with a new hairdo, new clothes and shoes and a new designer purse. People walking to and fro on the street instantly noticed Shay and began to greet her. Before she made it across the street to her friends, she'd had several conversations about her shoes, clothes and bag from admirers. In order to avoid more questions about her hair or whatever, Shay saw an opening and darted across the street to her friends. They all exchanged hugs and they began to kid her about her newfound celebrity.

"Chica, where you been?" Plena asked. "I know you ain't tryin' to act fake bougie."

"I do feel bougieness comin' offa her," Cat said. "Where you get that purse from? I just saw that in a Gucci catalog and it wasn't even out yet. How you got it?"

Shay was absolutely glowing in the spotlight. "They out if you know the plug. Trish what up? You just sittin' there lookin' crazy, what's wrong with you?"

"I'm good, Shay. What's poppin' with you? I see you ain't playing with these people. Hair done, nails done, new Adidas with the matching outfit. You is killin' em, Shay."

"Hell yeah!" Plena said loudly enough for Ace and his crew to hear. "My girl is tax refund clean and I know she ain't got no job. I hope don't none of these lames out here start hatin' neither, because ain't no love over here. Hashtag ain't no love."

Plena and Shay gave each other a high five as Shay asked, "Y'all ain't getting high?"

"Really, we busted, ain't no money," Cat explained. "We had one little bag of weed, but Mrs. Super Lungs Trish over here sucked up the blunt while we was runnin' our mouths. We been tryin' to get Ace and Swan to sponsor, but when they around they whole crew they got to act like they don't really get down with us like that. They got plenty of bottles over there and won't even give us a drink. Bet I won't be making no store runs for them no time soon."

"Oh, they tryna stunt?" Shay said as she reached into her purse and pulled out a fifth of Patron. She handed her purse to Trish. "Watch this. C'mon, Plena."

Clutching the bottle by the neck, Shay walked over to Ace and his guys. "What up with you ballers and shot-callers? 'Sup, Ace?"

Ace's crew's attention focused on Shay. There was a chorus of approving comments as they checked Shay out.

Ace looked around first before he spoke. "Waddup, Shay. Gone now, you know my baby mama out here."

Shay laughed. "Ace you is doing way too much. Ain't nobody thinking 'bout you or yo' baby mama. I thought ballers didn't have basic chicks anyways. Too bad, so sad. But I'm not on any of that, I'm just trying to get some cups and ice so we can pop our bottle. And if y'all throw in some of that lime juice we'll appreciate it."

As Ace's friends scrambled to fulfill Shay's order from their supplies, a group of loud custom motorcycles made their way down the street. While everyone's attention was on the motorcycles, over by Cat's car, Trish slipped her hand into Shay's purse and cuffed some drugs and cash. Shay thanked Ace's crew and made sure she rolled her eyes at him long and hard before she walked away. She and Plena returned to their friends. Plena opened the Patron and handed them all cups so she could pour them some drinks. Trish didn't accept her drink cup though. Instead, she hopped down from her perch on the car and handed Shay back her purse.

"That's a real nice purse, Shay," Trish said. "Aye, y'all, I'm finta bounce. My OG just called me. I'm finta go to the crib so I don't have to hear her mouth, I'm already on punishment. I don't want no more time added on my sentence."

"You sure, because we about to get high as gas prices," Shay said. "It's on me, too."

"Yeah, I'm sure Shay, I gotta get outta here. I'ma check y'all later."

As Trish walked off, Shay dug into her purse and pulled out some weed. She had begun to roll the weed when her cell phone alerted her that she had a new text message. She passed the unfinished blunt to Cat to continue rolling. The text message was from Ace.

Ace: GO HOME

Shay: Not tonite Im on the block

Ace: Do it look like Im playn

Shay: Take yo BM n go home goofy

Shay put her phone in her purse and turned to see Plena had a puzzled look on her face as she took a sip of her drink.

"Something ain't right," Plena said suspiciously. "Y'all see how Trish just left? I ain't never seen her pass up no free high. Never! Her mama could have been hanging from that streetlight right there and she still would have snuck and hit the weed. I know she was just as broke as us so she wasn't on nothing. What you say, Cat?"

Cat finished rolling the first blunt and passed it to Shay. "Yeah, that was weird. I ain't never seen that happen before. That girl know she love to get high and what's really crazy is she said her momma called her. On what? She ain't had no phone for a month now.

Plus, we was all right here, we would have seen her on the phone."

Plena sipped her drink as she seemed to be lost in thought for a few moments. "I'm for real y'all, I don't get it. Trish a baby hype, she don't turn down no high. Lately she been getting superman high, too. I heard she be smokin' that Scottie mess, too. She be going on 93rd over there with my cousin and nem. My cuzzo and them wild, too. They be smokin' dipped blunts with coke on 'em. On the dead, my cousin told me Trish be over there getting high like it's no tomorrow. Somethin' just ain't right y'all. Don't no cluck turn down no free high. Shay wasn't she holding your purse while we went to get some cups and ice? Check yo purse, Shay."

Shay placed her drink on the roof of the car, where it almost fell over, she caught it and handed it to Cat as she took a quick inventory of her purse. "Oooouuuu, she ppppeeetttyyyy! She got some mollies and like $16 that was Pat change from when I went to the store for her earlier."

Plena gulped her drink. "Let's go beat her down like the clucker she is. I can't stand a thief!"

At first Shay was with it, but when she took an inventory of her new clothes and accessories, she gave it a second thought. She went in her bra and fished out a wad of 100 dollar bills. She handed Plena and Cat both a couple of hundred dollars.

"Forget Trish for tonight," Shay said smoothly with a blunt hanging out the corner of her mouth. "I should thank her, she just saved me some money. I was gone put a few dollars in her pocket just like I hit y'all, but she took what she thought she had coming off the top. Plus, if she would have hung around, she'd have seen I got a way for us to never be broke again." Shay put the rest of her money back in her sports bra and reached in her purse. She pulled out a handful of drugs out of another compartment in her purse. "What she got wadn't nothing, we finta ball! I'm the plug now."

Instantly, Plena became paranoid. "Girl, put that up! You gone get us robbed out here with all these pill heads walking around. Don't think for one minute that these thirsty Negroes wouldn't poke us, too."

"She ain't lying, Shay," Cat agreed looking around. "Girl, put that up."

Shay put the drugs back into her purse and pulled out her gun. "I ain't worried about them, ain't nothing over this way but free smoke. They can run up if they want to. They know who my cuzzo is and my little brothers. We about to get to the money. We about to run our numbers up and be sitting on some paper before they even realize what happened. Y'all with me?"

Shay held her cup up. Plena and Cat looked at one another. Cat shrugged and touched her cup to Shay's.

"I don't care," Cat said. "I'm sick of being broke any way. This-a-way when my guy get out, I can help him get back on his feet."

Plena touched her cup to theirs. "Well, one thing y'all gotta know is we still gotta beat Trish ass when we catch her. On God, I'm personally kicking her in her forehead for being on that. It's like my granny said, you can't trust a chick with dirty Air Force Ones and no edges or something like that."

They all laughed at Plena's comment, and for awhile they were content to laugh and joke with one another as they drank and smoked their weed. The night was full of life as both young men and women walked by the girls sitting on Cat's car. Quite a few of them noticed how fly Shay was dressed. She received plenty of compliments and several men openly flirted with her. From a distance, Ace was seething as he kept a watchful eye on her. Shay continued to ignore him, as she made sure to twerk several times extra hard to the music being played in the background.

Ace wanted to, but he couldn't approach Shay for being disrespectful because his baby's mama had joined him and his friends. Eventually, Ace walked off with her, all the while casting poisonous looks in Shay's direction. Shay dismissed him with a wave.

Cat grabbed her arm. "You better quit showing out."

"He better go home to his family, before I have that basic chick big mad at him," Shay replied as she kept dancing. "Matter of fact he can ride home on her wide back."

Shay and her friends were laughing as Nayshawn and Jayshawn walked up. They were both wearing brand new outfits and shoes.

"What so funny?" Jayshawn asked as he picked up Plena's drink.

Plena snatched her cup, managing to spill most of it. "Well, if it ain't the killer kids," she said sourly, wringing the alcoholic liquid from her hand.

"What you say, Plena?" Nayshawn asked as he

hugged Cat.

"You heard me, Bangout Twins."

"Shay, you need to tell yo' friend to mind her business before she find herself in something she can't get out of," Jayshawn warned.

"She ain't gotta mind her business," Shay said. "What you two bugs want?"

"We don't want nothing, we just wanted to holler at our big sister," Jayshawn said innocently as he reached for Shay's drink, which she deftly maneuvered out of his reach.

"Hmph, I never see my little brothers unless they want something."

Jayshawn held up an empty cup. "Damn man, we can't have a drink with our big sis? We was just trying to see what was up with you. I know you ain't trying to go on us because you all fly."

Nayshawn took the blunt from Cat and Shay took it from him. "Y'all is irra, little brothers. Y'all don't be coming to get me when y'all got weed and drinks. And by the way, y'all is fly too, courtesy of me, so gone on because y'all blowing my high. Shouldn't y'all be in the house?"

"I know the Bangout Twins ain't gotta be in the house," Plena said sourly. "The cute little twins is now full grown killers."

Nayshawn got in Plena's face. "Stop playing with us before we forget you Shay's shadow and do you dirty." Plena jumped down off the car. "Boy, I don't care what you done did in these streets. I used to wipe yo' nose and put you to sleep. Now, throw another threat and

I'm gone get yo new clothes dirty for you. Then, you gone have to go and get yo' gun, because I know you can't fight, Nay. You might got all these lames around here scared of you, but I know better."

Nayshawn stood toe-to-toe with Plena, his anger smoldering. As he clenched and unclenched his fist, he appeared to want to hit Plena, but something about her defiance and absence of fear made him seem to think better of it, so he allowed Jayshawn to easily pull him away from her.

"Gone now, Plena," Jayshawn said. "We ain't even on that, you like our sister too. But just so you know, we ain't got to run and get nothing, we keep them on us. But, like I said, we ain't on that. We came to see what was up with Shay. The streets is talking. They saying she got it. We come to see can we get some."

Shay took a sip of her drink. "Y'all better gone. I ain't got nothing for y'all, I done already gave y'all some bread and bought y'all clothes and shoes. Beat it, I'm trying to chill."

Nayshawn said, "Come on, Shay-Shay, we see you shining. Let yo' little brothers get some of that light."
As Shay looked at her younger twin brothers, her face softened a bit. "Hold on," she said. She handed her cup to Jayshawn to free up her hands. He instantly took a sip and handed it to his twin to take a sip as Shay dug into her purse. She handed them both some pills and weed. She retrieved two 100 dollar bills from her bra and gave them each a bill.

"That's it, nah gone. Y'all ain't get it from me neither if Pat catch y'all high. I ain't playing neither."

The twins ran off like little kids with their newfound treasures.

"Didn't even say thanks, I tell you, Pat's kids is some straight savages," Shay said.

"They been out here wildin', Shay," Plena said matter-of-factly. "I'm gone tell you later."

Plena motioned with her head and Shay looked up to see Swan and several of his friends joining them.

"What's up with it, Shay?" Swan asked with a smirk.

Shay replied dryly, "What up, Swan. Please don't come tellin' me what yo' boy said if he can't come say it himself. He can save that for his other side chicks. I'm not on any of that."

"So, what you saying? You ain't with my guy?"

"He left with his girl didn't he? He dead. He left me on the curb with my bags because of that big back bum. A real one woulda let her know I'm dropping my peoples off, I aint'finta leave them out here like this. I ain't finta keep talking about this though. What you want, Swan?"

Swan laughed. "Nothing, Shay, just tryna see is you done switched up and started acting shady since you got on. Don't forget we rappies."

"Gone head with that, Swan. Don't be tryna gas me up, I ain't on."

"Nall, I'm just playing. I really do gotta holla at you about some business. It's about some bread, girl. For real, for real. Gimme yo number." Swan offered his cell phone to Shay to put her number in. Shay hesitated for a moment, then she took it and punched in her number. Swan took his phone back and locked her number in. "I'm gone hit you later. Right now we finta walk through and see what we can see. C'mon y'all."

Swan and the guys trooped off and Shay, Cat and Plena continued their get high session.

"P, what was you finta tell me earlier?" Shay asked.

Plena looked puzzled. "What is you talking about? I don't even remember. This weed fie than a mug. I forgot what we was even talking about."

"Something about my little brothers. You do remember Jay and Nay, don't you? You was just about to tell me something about them when Swan and nem walked up."

Plena was extremely animated, when she exclaimed, "Oh, yeah, Shay! Girl the twins is out here bad. The streets is saying that was them that kilt them people on Snipes Day. Not one, not two, but three."

"Who saying that?" Shay snapped. "And why is you repeating some he say, she say stuff?"

"Girl don't get mad at me, I ain't saying it. The twins is saying it. They be clout chasing on social media. They on Youtube calling theyselves the Bangout Twins."

"You have got to be kidding me," Shay said, her voice full of disbelief. "You cannot be serious. Cat you know about this, too?"

Cat nodded her head. "I just saw the video earlier. I tried to call you, but you wasn't answering yo' phone. They is actually doin' numbers on they video even though it's bootleg. They gettin' they views up. It's called Ain't No Love."

"I'm finta beat they butts!" Shay fumed. "They done lost they minds! They out here shootin' people! Wait 'til I tell Pat. C'mon, we finta find them."

The girls took their drinks and made their way through the crowd up and down the two block radius of the party. They looked in every vehicle, on every porch, every dice game, and group of males as they searched for the twins to no avail. By the end of their search, Shay was so aggravated she was ready to go.

"I'm finta go to the crib and see if they there. I'ma see y'all."

Plena and Cat took turns hugging before Shay walked away. Before she left, Shay topped off their cups with Patron and gave them plenty of weed.

CHAPTER 14

Trish stopped running when she made it several blocks from where she'd been partying with her friends. She ended up on 76th Street across the street from the neighborhood park. It was bordered by the park field house and the neighborhood high school. The night was relatively warm, so there were plenty of kids and young adults between the playground, basketball court and park benches.

After wiping dirt off a park bench, Trish plopped down and pulled her score out of her pocket to inspect it. Mentally, the whole time she was making her escape, her mind was racing. When she opened her hand, the first thing she did was count the money.

Disappointed she tucked the sixteen dollars into her sock top. "You've got to be kiddin' me," she said aloud at the pitiful amount of money she'd stolen.

Next, she inspected the pills and found that she'd stolen about 20 Mollies. "Some Mollies. She doing all that stuntin and all she got is 16 bucks and some Mollies. She cappin'. If Cat wasn't sitting her slow self next to me, then I could have went all through her purse. She had to have more than this, this ain't nothin'. I'm right back where I started. I definitely ain't got enough to get me a Roman candle."

Disgusted at her meager haul, she sat back on the

bench and thought about the first time she'd had a Roman candle. It happened while she was hanging over east with Plena in Plena's cousin's neighborhood. The block was filled with everybody from the hood just kicking it on set for one of their homies who'd just gotten killed. Trish had found herself happy to just sip on a drink and smoke every blunt passed to her. All the while a young dreadhead wearing a red Polo shirt and matching hat, kept grinning at her. Finally, he slid up to her and asked had she ever had a Roman candle.

Dreadhead grinned as he produced what looked like a regular blunt. He let her light it and when she inhaled it was the best thing she'd ever tasted or smoked in her life by far. It wasn't until later she found out the ingredients of the Roman candle, it was weed, and raw cocaine in a PCP dipped blunt. She was the highest she'd ever been in her life, and Dreadhead had her by the elbow and leading her away when Plena noticed.

She remembered Plena pushing Dreadhead away, while shouting, "Let go of my friend! She don't know you! She ain't going nowhere with you!"

Trish was so high that even if she hadn't wanted to go with Dreadhead, she couldn't put up a fight and she let Plena steer her away from her newfound friend. She couldn't find her tongue at the time, but if she would've been able to talk, she would have told Plena that Dreadhead could take her to Afghanistan, if he had some more Roman candles. That night though, they left without further incident. Two days later she took the #4 Cottage Grove bus back over there, but this time without Plena. She thought it might be challenging, but she easily found Dreadhead, and it wasn't long before she was in his bedroom, smoking on a Roman candle.

This time Dreadhead let her smoke an entire Roman candle by herself. Every time she would try to hand it to him, he would decline. She shrugged her shoulders and kept on smoking until the whole thing was gone. Soon she found herself the highest she'd even been in her life. Several times she blacked out, and when she came to she was sitting on Dreadhead's twin bed totally naked. She couldn't remember taking off her clothes.

From that point, she could only remember flashes but she knew she started off with Dreadhead between her legs. Then she blacked out again, and during her blackout, Dreadhead seemed to transform. He still had dreads, but he seemed smaller and a little darker, and then he changed again. This time he was older and seemed to have grown a full beard and a bald head. His breath was horrible too, like it made her gag it was so disgusting. She would have thrown up if she had eaten that day. Just when she thought she couldn't take one second more of smelling his breath, her Dreadhead friend changed again, making her think she was really tweaking. His dreads didn't grow back and he was really, really heavy. He was so heavy that she thought the bed would break, but it was on the floor already. She could barely breathe under all of his weight, and just when she thought she was going to die, Dreadhead turned back into himself. Thankful her friend turned back into himself, she passed out.

When she woke up, the room was dark and she couldn't tell how much time had passed. She knew it had been awhile, because it was still daylight when she first came here with Dreadhead. She used the illumination from the streetlight streaming through the broken blinds on the window to find her clothes and get dressed. She left the bedroom and went downstairs to the living room. In the living room, Dreadhead and several of his friends were playing a video game. There were several handguns on the chipped coffee table. As Trish looked around the room at Dreadhead's friends, from their faces and the grins they wore, she easily put together what had happened in the bedroom. There was smaller Dreadhead, Beard and Mohawk with the terrible breath, and Really Heavy. She ran out the door with their laughter burning her ears and made sure she never went back to their neighborhood.

Trish had gotten to the point that she just wanted to be high all the time. She'd told her friends that her mother had taken her cell phone and that she was on punishment. The truth was she'd sold her cell phone a long time ago, and her mother had put her out over 2 months ago when she stole $200 out of her stepdaddy's wallet. She'd been staying with her aunt Fruity, who was nice, but she was half-blind and stayed drunk, something that her nasty boyfriend tried to capitalize on when he was always trying to touch her. If Trish was in the bathroom, he always "accidentally" barged in. She'd caught him sniffing her dirty panties more than once. Usually, she liked to be so high that by the time she went in the house she just passed out. Fruity's boyfriend didn't seem to like it when she was stretched out like a stone cold statue so he would just leave her alone.

Trish looked down at the baggie of Mollies in her hand. She decided to sell them, so she could scrounge up a real high. Just to make sure they were okay to sell, she swallowed two of them. While she waited for the Mollies to take effect, she lit a piece of cigarette she had in her pocket and sat back. In a few minutes she was thirsty so she walked over to the park water fountain; it wasn't working.

She left the park and crossed the street to a row of bungalow houses. She checked two houses before coming to the third, it had what she was looking for: a water hose connected to the outdoor spout. She turned the water on and drank and drank and drank from the hose, but she just couldn't seem to quench her thirst. Eventually, she was so full of water, she couldn't drink anymore, so she dropped the hose and left the yard.

As she was walking down the street, she realized how wet she'd gotten her clothes--she was soaked. She took off her shirt and leaned against a gate and wrestled her pants off. She fell twice taking her pants off, but soon she was on her way, though not before she hung her clothes neatly on the gate to dry. Wearing only her underwear, shoes and socks she walked past the park.

Nayshawn and Jayshawn were sitting with two of their friends on the top of the back of a park bench getting high.

"Yo, check this chick out," one of their friends said.

They all looked up in time to see Trish strolling by like she was fully dressed.

"Who is that?" Jayshawn asked. "I can't tell from here, is that a cluck?"

"I don't think so, she look young," their other friend said. "I can see that from here."

Nayshawn hopped off the bench. "C'mon y'all, let's check this out."

The four boys skipped and jogged until they crossed the street and caught up with Trish. Nayshawn got in front of her to stop her from walking.

"Aye, where you going with no clothes on?" Nayshawn asked.

Jayshawn had been looking her up and down and he instantly recognized Trish, one of Shay's friends.

"Trish, where you goin' naked?" Jayshawn asked.

"What's wrong with you? Where yo' clothes at, girl?"

"I'm goin' to get my clothes right now. I'm lettin' them dry. I need something to smoke. You got something to smoke?"

Nayshawn recognized Trish too, but a mischievous grin crept on his face. "Trish, we got something to smoke. What you'll give us for something to smoke?"

"All I got is some Mollies, Mollies, Mollies."

"Where are they?" Nayshawn asked.

"They're in my clothes. You can have some Mollies. I just want enough to get me a Roman candle. You can have the rest. They are strong, too. Mollies are strong. Mollies are strong. I really don't like Mollies, but I love Roman candles. All I need is something to smoke, something to smoke, smoke something."

Jayshawn reached out and touched her chest. Trish didn't flinch. Nayshawn rubbed her butt and she still didn't balk.

"We don't want no Mollies, but we'll work something out Trish," Nayshawn said as he took her by the hand. "Come on y'all, we goin' to the garage."

Meekly, Trish went along with the four boys on a short walk. They cut through a vacant lot and crossed the alley to a garage behind one of their friend's houses. The boy who lived at the address carried the key to the garage door on a string around his neck. He keyed the door open and they led Trish through the door. The inside of the garage was decorated like an apartment with a bed, a sofa, several chairs, a table, even a big back television.

There was a half-gallon of cheap vodka on the table which Trish picked up and took a long swallow from it like it was water. Rayshawn handed her a blunt and she took it to the face. She started twirling around in circles in the middle of the garage as she smoked the blunt and drank the vodka. Nayshawn sat at the table and rolled another blunt. He motioned for her to come closer to where he sat. When she came to get the blunt, he held it out to her, then pulled it back.

"I want to smoke," she whined. "Come on, let me smoke."

"You can smoke, but you gotta take off yo' underwear" Nayshawn said smoothly.

Trish stripped without the slightest hesitation. Nayshawn pulled her to stand between his legs while he sat in the chair and handed her the blunt.

Nayshawm leaned forward and wrapped his arms around Trish, as he stuck his head around her body. "Rest of y'all gotta get out. Since me and Jay know her, we gone chill with her first, then y'all can have her. And lock the door."

As their friends reluctantly trooped out, Nayshawn led Trish over to the bed.

CHAPTER 15

Shay was still steaming as she keyed herself into the apartment. She hoped her twin brothers were home so she could wild out on them. As she opened the door, she noticed a police detective's business card on the threshold. They must have slipped it under the door, she thought as she picked it up and peered at it.

"Pat! Pat!" she yelled. She went and opened the door to Pat's bedroom without knocking and saw that Pat wasn't there. Shay tossed the business card on Pat's dresser. She pulled out her cell phone and dialed Pat's number on her cell phone and waited for an answer.

Her mother picked up after a few rings. Without preamble, Shay asked, "Where you at, Pat? Are you coming home tonight? What do you mean? I can ask you that, you my mama and I want to know where you are. Alright, alright Pat, I don't want to hear all that. I needed my mother, but I'm good now. I done got used to you not being no help. Bye, Pat. Bye, Pat."

Shay went to her room and slung her purse and phone on her bed. She took her shoes off and went to the bathroom. When she came back in the room she got a blunt, and her phone and went out on the back porch for a smoke. She took a seat and as she lit her blunt she opened Facebook. She used her fake page to view Ace's baby mama's page. She liked a few of the pictures the girl posted with them looking like such a happy couple. She grinned as she thought about how hard it was going to be to look at his chubby baby mama after her next performance.

She scrolled through a few more of their pictures, even commenting: "Kaute" with heart emojis under the picture of their little funny looking baby. Tired of cyber-stalking, she was signing into her real page when she received a text from Swan.

Swan: Wyd?

Shay: Y?

Swan: Board just checking Stop being like that

Shay: Stop being like what?

Swan: Heartless Like we ain't people

Shay: We not people

Swan: What u want Swan?

Swan: 2 c u

Shay: U just saw me

Swan: Not like that U no

Shay: No, I don't kno

Swan: U no what I mean U was lookin all good and thick U at the crib by yoself Im trying to keep u company I no u ain't tripping on my boy Ace He at the crib with his bm Or his side chick Ace ain't thinking about u so I hope u ain't thinking about him

Shay: I kno I'm hi over here I must be tweakin becuz Swan ain't never throw his guy under the bus

Swan: Im just trying to see what's up with u

Suddenly Shay had an idea. It was a chance to get Swan back for what she thought may have happened the day she was drunk at his crib.

Shay: If u serious send me a pic of yoself down there If I like it we gone spend the nite 2nite

Swan: U serious? Im finta send that to u now

Within seconds a text alert let Shay know she'd received a picture. She opened the picture message and giggled. "I'm about to expose yo' sneaky butt. Let's see how much yo' guy Ace like this."

Shay posted the picture of Swan's privates on several social media sites, taking care to tag Ace in each post. Her caption read: Aint no love out here Disloyal homies send pix like this to they homie girl The thirst is real #heartlessinChicago

She couldn't help but laugh as the comments and likes started pouring in on her pages. In minutes, Ace and Swan started blowing up her phone, but she never answered. Her anger at her little brothers and Pat's less than stellar parenting was long gone as she sat on the porch, and smoked her blunt while playing games on her cell phone.

•••••

In his bedroom, Swan stopped trying to call Shay. He ignored a call from Ace as he went through the video archive in his cell phone. "Oh, she wanna flex, I'm gone show her how to flex. You gone learn 'bout playin' with Swan."

He found the video he was looking for of Shay and Ace having sex and posted it with the caption: Ain't no fun if the homie can't have none

Content at his revenge, Swan lay back on his bed and watched the views and comments as they began to post.

CHAPTER 16

An unmarked police car pulled into the high school parking lot. Detective Williams parked the vehicle in a slot reserved for vice-principals. He shut the car off, but didn't move. Farillo knew his partner all too well and noticed his hesitation.

Farillo asked, "You ready for this?"

"No," Williams said firmly. "I ever tell you how much I hate kids?

Det. Farillo laughed. "All the time. What about your stepkids?"

"Those two more than any others," Williams griped. Both detectives laughed.

Det. Williams lit a cigarette. "Farillo, you really think these two came to school today or any other day? Why would these teenage killers go to school? Your hunch better be right, Farillo, or you're buying lunch."

"Well, I figure we can't catch them at home so we might as well try these holding pens they call public high school."

The detectives exited their vehicle and walked around to the front of the high school to gain entrance. Inside the school, they displayed their badges to the security guard and he pointed them in the direction of the school's Main Office.

In the office, the two homicide detectives stood at

the counter and waited for the secretary to check the twins' attendance for the day using the computer on her desk. There were several employees in the office plus a male student waiting to see the principal.

The school secretary peered over her reading glasses at the computer screen. After scrolling through several pages, she said, "Detectives, it seems like both boys were in their division room this morning. That's actually been a rare occasion these days. They never were what you would call career students, but at least they used to try. Now, it's like they have given up. Either they are suspended or absent. It's…"

Det. Williams cut off her long-winded answer. "Ma'am where exactly are they right now? What class are they in?"

The school secretary looks at the clock, then back at the computer. "Nayshawn should be in Geography, room 217 and Jayshawn should be in the Wood shop. I'll page Officer Swinson, he'll have to accompany you to the rooms. And if they're taken into custody he actually has to put the cuffs on them and call for a transport. School policy. Just have a seat for a moment and I'll alert him. He'll be along shortly."

The detectives took a seat next to the student waiting to see the principal. The boy waited until the school secretary was immersed in a phone call, then slipped out of his chair and out of the office. They waited patiently, but after five minutes passed, Williams and Farillo were ready to tell the secretary to call for the school officer again, but then Officer Swinson walked into the office. The school secretary pointed him in the detectives' direction with a tilt of her head. Officer Swinson went over and shook hands with the detectives. Before they left the office, the school secretary handed Officer Swinson a post-it note with the twins' names and classrooms on it.

"This way gentlemen," Officer Swinson said cheerfully. "Let's see if we can corral our wayward students."

The detectives followed the school police officer out of the office. Now that the detectives were gone, the school secretary looked around for the student that was supposed to be waiting to see the principal.

"Now where the heck did Jamal go?" the school secretary said. "I swear that boy is slippery as an eel. Take your eyes off of him for a second and he's gone. Hope he just went to the washroom."

••••

Instead of being in class, Nayshawn and Jayshawn were with several friends in the cafeteria. Two schoolmates provided them with a beat by tapping pencils and beating on the lunchroom table as they rapped some of their new song, Heartless. One of their friends sitting next to the cipher was only halfway listening to the rapping, as he scrolled through his social media timeline on his cell phone. He stopped scrolling momentarily and his eyes got huge.

"Nay, check it out, boy," the boy with the phone said.

"Hold up, bro. I'm about to flow."

"Forget all that, you gone wanna see this," the boy said as he handed Nayshawn his phone.

Nayshawn accepted the phone. "It bet not be no

meme or nothing about Lebron James."

From his perch on the lunchroom table, Nayshawn looked at the video on his friend's phone. Within seconds his face distorted into an ugly mask of hate. He grabbed his friend by the collar.

"Man, who posted that?" Nayshawn growled. "Who posted that?!?"

The boy squirmed in Nayshawn's clutch. "I don't know homie, his name is Swan."

Nayshawn released the boy's collar and tossed the phone to his twin brother. "Bro, some dude named Swan done lost his mind. You know him?"

Jayshawn watched the video, soon he was so angry he was shaking. "Homie online talking crazy, too. Wait 'til we catch up with bro, I'm gone make sure he win a wet t-shirt contest."

Jayshawn handed the cell phone back to their friend. He said, "Aye, bro, type this: Bangout Twins said take it down."

Their friend followed the instruction and typed the demand. Shortly a reply comment posted: Tell the Bangout Twins they can have next gotta wait n line tho

"Yeah, he either crazy or high," Jayshawn said. "Oooouuuuu, we got him. He wanna try and expose somebody. I can't wait til we catch up to him and do some exposing of our own. Just wait."

Jamal, the boy from the school office knocked on the cafeteria's side door until a passing student pushed it open for him. Breathless, Jamal charged up to the twins.

"Twins, I been lookin' all over for y'all. Them people

is up here to arrest y'all."

"What? What you say?" Jayshawn asked.

Winded, Jamal put his hands on his knees. "Bro, homicide detectives was just in the office asking whether y'all was in school today. They told em yeah, one of y'all 'sposed to be in Geography and the other in Wood shop. I ran there first to look, but I ain't see y'all. I knew y'all was either in the gym or here, if y'all was still in school."

"Did they say what they was looking for us for?" Nayshawn asked.

Jamal looked at them like they'd lost their minds. He said, "Do it make a difference? Y'all need to get up out of here now and figure that out later, bro. If they tryna get up with y'all at school, then they thirsty. Y'all better bounce."

"You ain't lyin," Nayshawn asked. "Good lookin, Jamal. We out gang, ain't nobody seen us."

The twins grabbed their belongings and when the lunchroom monitor wasn't looking they slipped out of one of the fire exit doors. It triggered a short alarm, but they were gone before anyone could come investigate.

CHAPTER 17

Shay sat up in her bed. It took her a moment to recognize where she was as her bedroom came into focus. She squinted at the sun streaming through the ragged mini-blinds bunched in several sections. She started to get up, but groaned as she got halfway up and sat back down. She reached for her purse, but it wasn't where she left it. That made her jump up. She looked around her bed for her purse. It wasn't until she looked on her dresser that she noticed Pat leaning against the door jamb holding her purse.

Pat dangled her purse by the strap. "Looking for this?"

At first Shay seemed fearful, then she threw caution to the winds and strolled over and took her purse from Pat. She pulled out her pack of cigarettes and offered Pat one. With a strange look on her face, Pat took it. Shay lit both of their cigarettes and went to have a seat. Shay felt Pat's eyes on her, but she played it cool as she sat on her bed and smoked her cigarette.

For the first time in a long time, Pat wasn't her usual boisterous self. Shay couldn't figure out what the look on her mother's face meant, as Pat leaned her head against the wall and smoked her cigarette in silence.

Finally, Pat said, "The police is looking for yo' little brothers."

Shay played dumb. "For real, what they do?"

"They wanna talk to them about some murders. They just like they daddy! He was a killer, too. That Negro would kill somebody over anything. He tried to kill me a couple of times, he shot at me and choked me out before. All he did was gangbang, too. We couldn't do nothin' or go nowhere because he was always into it with somebody. Somebody was always shooting at him and he was shooting at them. That's alright, they gone end up just like him, in the morgue with their head blowed off."

While Pat was talking, Shay tried to inconspicuously take a look in her purse.

Pat noticed and told her, "All yo' stuff in there. I ain't no thief, you know I hate a thief. I was just taking a look at it, that bag is mean. I seen all that stuff in it, too. I ain't mad about you getting you some money, long as you ain't serving out my house. That weed you got any good?"

"Yeah, it's gas. OG Cali."

"I don't know what all that is. Is it fie?"

"Yeah, Pat." Shay dug into her purse and handed Pat a couple of bags. Pat handed her back one.

Pat said, "You may need that to buy me a bag like that for my birthday present. Ain't gotta be the exact one, but it gotta be good like that. You understand me?"

"I got you, Pat. I'm gone give you a few dollars, too after I run out this morning."

Pat opened the bag of weed and held it up to her nose to smell it. "You make sure you be careful out there, Shay. This new generation don't play fair and they won't hesitate to hurt you."

"Dag, Pat, you don't even sound heartless for once, and you called me by my name. You startin' to scare me."

Her remark drew a slight laugh from Pat, though there wasn't much mirth in the sound. "If you see your brothers tell them to stay away from here. That couple of dollars you was gone give me, give it to them. They need it more than me."

With that, Pat turned and left. Shay then picked up her phone. She saw that she'd missed calls and had a gang of text messages. She was scrolling through her call log when her cell phone rang. She looked at the caller ID, it was Plena, so she answered.

"What's up, squad? Nah, I ain't been on IG. I'm just getting up. Just now. Girl, calm down, you talking too fast. Swan did what? Look, let me call you back. I said I'm gone call you back, I'm finta look at it. Okay."

Shay ended her call with Plena and immediately logged onto her social media. She quickly found the video of herself having sex with Ace. Instantly, she knew when it happened and could tell that someone, probably Swan, snuck and shot the footage of them. At first she was furious, but as she scrolled through the comments under the video she saw how many people were condemning Swan's actions for trying to expose her as cowardly. A lot of people were not only dissing him, but they were for the most part saluting her. She checked her page and they were hundreds of inbox messages and over 500 friend requests.

"Damn, my inbox is bussin' and friend requests is crazy. That goofy ain't do nothin' but put me in my glow tryin' to get clout off me! All he did was clout me up!"

She called Plena back. "Yeah, I saw it. Swan big mad because I posted his little peter-weter. He called me last nite tryin' to put dirt on Ace name, hoping I would spend the night with him. I might be heartless, but I don't get passed around the crew. Never! On no day. I'm finta come get up with you anyway. I just gotta shower and I'm in the streets. Call Cat and tell her I said pull up, I got gas money."

Shay hung up her phone and went to take a shower. As she walked past Pat's room to go to the bathroom, she could smell weed. She smiled as she went into the bathroom.

CHAPTER 18

Ace pulled into a parking spot in front of Swan's grandmother's house. He turned the loud music down and cut his car off. He got out of the car and pulled out his cell phone. He called Swan and received no answer. He looked up at Swan's bedroom window and he could have sworn that he saw the curtains move. He reached into the car and blew three short blasts on the car horn. He tried calling Swan again; no answer.

To Swan, Ace texted: I know u n da crib Come outside You kno Granny will let me n

Seconds later, Swan texted: Comin down

Ace walked over and sat on the porch. For the five minutes it took for Swan to come out of the house, Ace played a zombie killing game on his phone. Swan came onto the porch carrying a bowl of cereal.

"Waddup, bro? You out early." Swan said between spoonfuls of cereal.

"What you on Swan? You sendin' pics like that to my chick, bro?"

"For real Ace? For real? You really questioning me about a chick that ain't yo woman, bro? You over here early in the morning in yo' feelings about a eater, bro?"

Ace dismissed that with a wave of his hand. "Ain't nobody in they feelings. You kill me. Always tryin' to holla that somebody in they feelings. Gone with that! I been messin' with Shay since she was 13 and you know it, boy. And, I ain't never gave her more than a high or a French fry. How I'm in my feelings?"

Swan drank the remainder of milk from his cereal bowl before answering, "Boy, you at my granny crib early in the morning. You was blowin' up my phone last night. You gotta be feelin' some type of way, my dude."

Ace laughed, but it was forced. "I ain't tryna to hear that. All I'm saying is that if you want Shay or any one of my side chicks, you gotta holla at me first. So, quit tryna to make it seem like I'm in my feelings."

"You sound like you in love, on God" Swan asked. "Because I swear I done let you crack plenty of my chicks before. You seem to forget that your baby mama that you live with was mine. I let you get down with her because you said you was feelin' her so I backed off. I cut off all contact, but here it is you at my Granny crib early in the a.m. about Shay?"

"I'm telling you, I ain't trippin' about Shay. That ain't my BM or nothin'. I'm trippin' about you postin' the video. The timing wasn't right. It makes us look like we lames or something."

"Man, they can act like they don't know," Swan said. "We been taking down they girls for years now. They know we ain't thirsty. I didn't do it for no clout, neither. I popped some X last night and the chick I had plans with, her brother came and got her to make her go home. Shay was looking good earlier and you ain't want her, so I shot my shot. She stunted on me, so I posted the video."

Nayshawn stepped out of the gangway on the side of the house holding a .357 pistol. Jayshawn came from the other end of the porch with a .380 semi-automatic pistol.

"Speakin' of shootin' your shot," Nayshawn said with a wicked smile. "Wassup now? Told you the Bangout Twins would be to see y'all."

Ace realized that they were boxed in, but he decided to try and play it cool. "Sup little homies, what's good?"

Jayshawn walked over to Ace and Swan and checked the waistlines of both boys for weapons. "What you think is good and you got that video up of my sister on the net? What would be good with you if that was yo' sister? You wouldn't have no problem with that, buddy?"

Ace was silent, but all the while he cast sideways glances at Swan.

Jayshawn said, "Why you keep looking at him? I asked you a question. How would you feel if that was yo' sister that you loved? Would you be angry?"

"I wouldn't like it," Ace said. "But, I didn't post it and I didn't make her do nothing she didn't want to do. Facts"

"Y'all two be together so it don't make a difference which one of y'all posted it," Jayshawn commented. "You may not love your sister if you got one, but we love ours and we ain't finta see nobody do her wrong. Especially, not for likes on Instagram and Facebook."

"It wasn't even like that," Swan protested. "I wasn't trying to get no likes and views. She exposed me and I posted the video. I wasn't thinking…"

"That's right, you wasn't thinking!" Nayshawn said, pointing his pistol at Swan. "Now, as I can recall we asked you to take it down earlier. You basically said we need to get in line or somethin', you meant that, homie?"

Swan visibly gulped. "I ain't know who you was little homie. If I knew it was you, I would have been took it down. Let me take it down right now, bro? I can take it down right now."

"Yeah do that for me, go head homie, take it down," Jayshawn said.

Swan's hands were visibly shaking as he deleted the video from his social media pages.

"Hurry up," Nayshawn snarled.

"It's done," Swan announced and handed his phone to Nayshawn.

Nayshawn looked at the cell phone and put it in his pocket. He motioned to Ace with his pistol. "Phone, boy. Empty them pockets, too. We need that cash, run them chains, and pull them belts. You, Mr. Get In Line, take off yo shirt and wrap everything up in there."

"I swear y'all is movin' way too slow for me," Nayshawn threatened. "If I have to hurry y'all, y'all ain't gone like it."

Hurriedly, Ace and Swan took off their belongings and put them in Swan's shirt. They handed the shirt bundle to Nayshawn.

"Don't let nothin' like this happen again, cause next time ain't no talkin'," Jayshawn threatened. "Y'all lucky y'all gettin' out this one without gettin' wet up."

Jayshawn and Nayshawn left the yard and were

about to walk away when Jayshawn turned around and caught Ace glaring at them with a hateful look. Ace tried to make his face go blank, but it was too late. Jayshawn put his hand on his twin's arm to stop him from walking away.

To Nayshawn, Jayshawn said, "Hold up, bro. I think we may have a problem." Jayshawn walked back into the yard and addressed Ace. "Man, homie you got a look on yo' face like you wanna do somethin'. This ain't no rap video, this for real boy."

Ace put his hands up. "Y'all got it, young bulls. Y'all did what y'all did, ain't nothin' we can do about it."

"What's that 'sposed to mean?" Nayshawn asked.

Ace mumbled something unintelligible under his breath. Swan put his hand on Ace's arm to try to silence him.

"C'mon bro leave it alone," Swan said. "They got that little stuff, let them gone they way."

Jayshawn's smile returned to his face. "Ain't that cute, homie trying to keep his man calm. Let him go. He can say what he want to say, its gravy. Say what you gotta say."

Ace shrugged Swan's hand off his arm and looked at Jayshawn long and hard, then he threw caution to the winds. "How you little chumps robbing us like you don't know me? On my baby, I used to give yo' sister money to buy y'all ice cream and now y'all pull this? Y'all goin' too far. Y'all lucky I ain't got my gun…"

"Or what?" Nayshawn growled. "You what? Move Jay! I ain't finta play with these boys!"

Nayshawn pushed past his brother, raised his pistol

and shot Ace several times in the chest. Jayshawn shrugged and shot twice, blasting Swan off of his feet. He stood over Swan and shot him six more times. Swan's grandmother opened the door of the house and looked out, but Nayshawn let off a shot at her, sending her scurrying back inside. The twins looked up and down the block and then jogged off.

CHAPTER 18

Dee removed her ear buds and lifted the small plastic blind on the airplane window. She hated flying in the smaller cheaper airplanes of the budget airlines, but sometimes depending on where you were coming from, and where you were going to, they were usually the first thing smoking out of some of the smaller less traveled cities.

She had just departed from Boise, Idaho, a place she never had any desire to visit for any reason except, to get to the money. It was a bit of a risk going to places like Idaho, Wyoming, and Montana because Black people were definitely in the minority in places like these. But, also because of their rarity, white peoples' mistrust wasn't as acute and they would hand over envelopes full of money to a pretty woman with a smile. Que usually accompanied her, but he said he wasn't feeling too good, so Dee went to take care of the business by herself.

The good thing was, because Boise was such virgin territory when it came to scamming, that instead of the usual 3-4 days it took for things to go through, this time it cleared in only 2 days. The minute she got the all clear from the bank, Dee rushed and drained the account and was headed for the airport 2 days ahead of schedule. She had talked to Que earlier in the day, he said he was feeling better and had gone to get breakfast and was going to run a few errands. When Dee tried calling him with the good news about the quick turnaround on their scam he didn't answer. She figured he must have left his phone in the car or at home while he was running errands so she didn't keep calling.

The flight home wasn't too long and it was uneventful, actually boring. There was no in-flight movie and the guy snoring loudly two rows behind Dee made certain that no one else in the immediate vicinity would get any sleep. She decided to have a drink to pass the time, but the stewardess informed her that they were out of wine. She didn't want any whisky, so it was a dry flight for her. Now, as she looked out the window and could clearly see Chicago, she was filled with a mixture of relief and happiness. As the plane banked to prepare to land, Dee thought about the $33,000 in her purse and how happy it would make Que. He had appeared to finally accept the terms of their business arrangement and he'd actually been more pleasant as of late.

It felt like things were getting back to normal slowly, but surely. They still weren't being intimate, but she had begun to blame it on all the drugs he ingested daily. She was thinking about giving him this whole score minus expenses for himself; maybe that would help his disposition.

The plane landed. Dee got her small carryon bag from the overhead bin and made tracks for the airline terminal. She ordered an Uber ride on her cell phone on the way. In the back of the Uber car, she almost had the driver stop twice to get some flowers and chocolate, but she quickly pushed those romantic thoughts out of her head. She wanted Que to remember why he fell in love with her, but she didn't want to push the issue. They had been together since she was fifteen and illegal, and she had even defied her mother, Pat, to be with him.

In the back of her mind she could remember how frustrated Pat was with her for being in love with a grown man. She could actually recall Pat telling her that he was gonna get tired of her one day. She didn't want to admit it, but maybe Pat was right. She used to hate when Pat called her a goofy sucker. Pat wanted her to be heartless too, but it wasn't easy when she used to stare into Que's hazel eyes. He always smelled so good and the boys she was used to being around always smelled musty or like puppies. The boys from her neighborhood were so clumsy, harsh and stupid. Que on the other hand was smooth as silk and took her places and bought her clothes and fed her good food.

Boys her age were no competition for a man like Card Crackin' Que, as they called him. Then, before she knew it, she was sixteen and pregnant. Of course Que wanted her to get rid of it, but she'd hid her pregnancy from him and Pat for so long, by the time they found out, the baby was moving around in her stomach. Even Pat had to agree that it was too late to have an abortion, and she ended up having Honey, her first daughter. Que's family, his mother, aunts, and four sisters all but took the baby away from Dee. That was good because Pat had sworn long ago that she was done raising kids and she was serious. She really didn't even raise Jayshawn and Nayshawn, Dee and Shay had them more than her.

The Uber car pulled up in front of their building. She grabbed her bag, tossed the driver a tip and got out of the car. After a short elevator ride to the 34th floor, she keyed open the apartment door and stepped inside. She set her carryon bag inside the hallway closet and went into the bedroom looking for Que. Good, she thought. He hasn't made it back. She took the envelope of cash out of her purse and went into the closet. She opened several Christian Louboutin shoeboxes looking for her sexiest pair of red bottoms. Her plan was to grab the shoes and hop in the shower, and hopefully Que didn't come in while she was in the shower; if he did, she planned to improvise.

S he found the shoes she was looking for and was about to leave the closet when she heard a noise. Dee turned off the closet light and with a smile on her face she peeked through the half opened door as she prepared to surprise Quincy.

The smile dropped off her face when she saw that Quincy was not alone; he was kissing and hugging a girl younger than her. He led the girl over to their bed.

"I don't like being here, Que," the girl said with a nervous giggle. "I know this is your place, but every since yo' baby mama been stayin' here I don't like comin' here. I don't know how I let you finesse me to comin' here again."

In total shock, Dee watched as Que was all over the

woman, kissing and touching her. As she watched the scene from the closet, it felt surreal, like it couldn't really be happening, but she knew it was.

Between kisses, Quincy said, "Princess, my BM is outta town 'til day after tomorrow taking care of my business. She don't run nothing no way. I just let her stay here because she ain't have no place to go and I ain't want my baby over her mama messed up crib. That's the problem, I moved that bum in here and she started thinking she a boss. I got something for her though. I'm finta take my shorty and bounce to Houston."

Princess stood up on the bed over Que and put her foot on his chest. "What about me, Que? You gone leave me here while you go to Houston? I thought I was your bae. You was sayin' you don't want to live without me the other day."

Que rubbed Princess' shapely leg. "I'm taking you with me to take care of us. I'm gone take the bread she been stacking. Since she think she a boss now she gone have her chance to start from the bottom like one. I'm gonna rent us a house, and you can get in nursing school like you wanted. I'm gone pay for it, too."

"That's what I really want to do," Princess said, as she clapped her hands together like a child. "Thank you, baby! I want to take care of us and you know I want to go to nursing school because I'm smart. The teachers used to tell me that in school all the time."

"I bet they did," Quincy said as he pulled her down to kiss him.

In the closet, Dee could hear their kissing sounds

as she reached onto a shelf and took down a shoebox that contained a pistol. She sat on the floor and began loading the gun. When she was finished, she got to her feet, said a short prayer, crossed herself, and was on her way out the closet when her phone vibrated with a picture of her daughter on the screen. She ignored the call and put her phone away, but her daughter called again. And again. And again. Though she didn't answer, the calls from her daughter brought her back to reality and she realized that she was just about to commit a double murder. She put the pistol down and did some calming exercises with her hands while taking deep breaths. As she calmed down, Dee crept back over to the closet door and waited for them to finish. She had decided against murdering them both, but she definitely was going to pop out the closet and put her hands on Princess.

In her childlike voice, Princess asked, "Do you think your B.M. gone make trouble? Try to get you locked up for kidnappin' or somethin'?"

"I already got that figured out. She can't do none of that from the fed joint. I'm gone send her off to Wyoming or somewhere to bust a move. Then, I'm gone put the people on her. I'm gonna tell her it's her first move on her own and she can have everything. I guarantee that greedy broad gonna go for it. One simple call to the federal bank fraud hotline and she can cancel Christmas. Meanwhile, back at the ranch, I grab the cash, call the movers, and we outta here."

"What about your daughter?" Princess asked.

"Oh yeah, she not gonna come down to Houston

at first. She gone be with my mama and nem 'til I get everything situated."

As Dee thought about how easily the man she loved was talking about betraying her, it made her sink back into a pile of dirty clothes. A tear escaped her eye, but she wiped it away. In her mind, she replayed all the things Pat had told her about Que and how anybody that lies and steals for a living couldn't be trusted. Her lip began to quiver as she thought about everything she'd went through to be with him. Unable to hold her tears back any longer, Dee climbed into the pile of clothes and sobbed until she fell asleep.

Later, she stood over the sleeping forms of her child's father and his teenage lover. She pointed her fingers like a gun at them before she left the room. In the building's parking garage, she sat behind the steering wheel of her car in total shock at the things she'd just overheard and witnessed. She now knew why Pat always told her never love a man more than you love yourself. The more she thought about it, the angrier she got. She had given up her childhood for Que, dropped out of high school, and stayed away from her family for him. After all the loyalty she'd shown, the minute he found some new young girl, he was ready to get rid of her. Now she was angry with herself that she didn't pull the trigger.

Stop being weak, you 'sposed to be heartless, she told herself.

As she was sitting in her car trying to figure out her next move, her cell phone vibrated. She looked at the display; it was her favorite cousin Dazo. She started not to answer, but on instinct, she did.

"Dazo, what's up cuz?" Dee said. "Y'all are where? Cuz, I need to talk to you, run something by you. Okay, I know where that park is at, I'm finta slide on you now. I'll be there in about 10, 15 minutes. Okay."

Dee ended the call and drove out of the parking garage. Twenty minutes later, she arrived at the park her cousin hung out in every day. The parking lot was packed and it took her a few minutes to find a parking spot. Finally, someone left a space. She pulled into it and exited her vehicle. There were many groups of people littering the parking lot, drinking, and smoking. She walked past them to a small group of spectators watching a pickup basketball game in the park. She spoke to several of the men and hugged her cousin, Dazo.

"Dazo, what's popping, cuz?"

"Waddup, cuz," Dazo said by way of greeting. "Good to see you cousin. You lookin' good, even if you don't sound too good. Somebody done had my cousin cryin' too, my favorite cousin at that. I'm really gonna need to know who makin' my cousin cry. Now, see, we out here celebratin' my homie beating his case and now I'm gone have to catch a case. What's going on, cuzo? Holla at me."

Dee looked around at her cousin's friends, they were all staring interestedly. She knew down to the last man they were loyal soldiers to her cousin, but she felt self-conscious about airing her dirty laundry in front of them. "Check it out, cuz," Dee said.

Dazo adjusted the newspaper under his arm as

they walked off a-ways from his guys. It took several minutes, but Dee explained the whole reason for her tears to him.

"And now this clown wanna set you up with the feds so he can live happily ever after with his little concubine?" Dazo asked in total disbelief. "This Negro is super disrespectful and he gots to go! He couldn't never think he was gone do this to my family and get away with it. He trippin' hard. Really, all you did was try to get y'all bread up and this what he do? I told you dude was moist. That's crazy!" Dazo showed Dee the small machine gun he was carrying in the newspaper under his arm. "What's up cuz, you ready to let me do me? You say the word and me and my young bulls will be on his heels. I never did like fam anyway, he always struck me as being too slick for his own good."

"Nall cuz, shootin' him is too easy. I could have shot him myself, I almost did. If it wasn't for my daughter I would have blasted him and his little girlfriend! They was in the bed that I sleep in, plotting on me. I ain't trying to spend the rest of my life in the joint, though. What's crazy is Pat told me about him, over and over, but my goofy self was in love. He was my first and couldn't nobody tell me nothin' about him, neither."

"Sounds like you still on that love train, cuz," Dazo said decidedly. "You won't let us burn him. I tell you, ain't nothing like a sucking chest wound to get his mind right, Dee."

Dee laughed nervously. "I imagine so, cuz. I'm far from being in love right now, though. Believe me, I'm heartless right now. I'm gone put him out of his misery myself, but I want to do it with finesse. I don't want him dead, well not yet anyway, but I do want to teach him a lesson."

"I got it," Dazo said.

Dee waved him off. "Nall cuz, I told you, I don't want you and your trigger-happy guys to do nothin'. Y'all will be done shot me and my daughter."

"Nall, nall cuz, I got something else, Dee. Do you remember I was telling you to watch out for mickeys, the pills they be slipping in people's drinks to mess them up?"

"Yeah, you was telling me to watch out for them in the club."

Dazo grinned. "You say you want to do him dirty without killin' him right? Check this out. This chemist I know was trying to make a new and improved date rape drug, don't ask, but something was wrong with the formula. What he ended up with is totally untraceable in the bloodstream, but it fries the brain. Out to lunch permanently. Does that sound like something you could use to get even?"

Dee smacked her hands together. "On my baby, that's exactly what I need. Call yo' guy right now. I want to buy a couple."

"You ain't gotta buy nothin', cuz," Dazo said. "I got a couple, I'm gone give 'em to you. These a gift from me. Hang tight while I send for those."

Dazo signaled one of his guys over and whispered in his ear. After receiving instructions, his guy ran off. Dazo and Dee rejoined his guys watching the hoopers while they waited for his guy to return. The runner returned shortly and slipped something into Dazo's hand. Dazo indicated for Dee to follow him and he walked with her to her car in the parking lot before giving her the package. There were two innocent looking pills with hearts stamped on them in a small plastic baggie.

"Cuz, listen up. You got to be careful with these Dee. They may not look like much but they do their job. Far as I know there's no coming back from these either, so you make sure that's what you really wanna do."

Dee put the pills in the inside pocket of her purse. She gave her cousin a huge hug and used her keyless entry to unlock her vehicle. She started her car, put her vehicle in gear and reversed out of the parking space.

"Cuz, promise me you gone be careful with them joints," Dazo called out.

"I got this, cuz," Dee answered before zooming away.

Dazo watched her car depart the parking lot before turning to rejoin his buddies watching the basketball game. As he walked, he glanced inside the folded newspaper at his machine pistol. "I ain't gone never get a chance to shoot somebody with you," he grumbled.

CHAPTER 20

Plena, Cat, and Shay laughed and joked with one another as they walked down the hallway of their high school between classes. Their clothes and shoes had been upgraded, and their classmates noticed how fly the girls looked. The three friends were all but basking in the attention of their fellow students. All of the boys' attention was focused on them as well, especially on Shay. She knew all the attention was mostly because of the clip of her private time with Ace, but she had also taken care to dress extra fly today. In her mind, as she walked the school hallways, it felt like she was famous or was starring in her own music video. She flirted and tossed her expensive sew-in hair around like she was a movie star.

As they rounded a corner with a small entourage following them, Trish was getting some things out of her locker. She didn't see her friends until it was too late to escape into a classroom or down a corridor.

Shay spotted her first. "Look y'all, here go y'all little clucker friend with the sticky fingers."

While their harsh laughter rained down upon her ears, Trish picked up her bookbag, but she wouldn't look Shay in the eyes. With her head down, she mumbled, "I didn't even steal yo' money or yo' pills, Shay."

"You so dumb," Shay said while shaking her head. "I ain't said nothing about no money and pills missing. How you knew that? Did one of y'all say something about what was missing to her?"

Plena got right up in Trish's face and grabbed her by her dingy collar. "Nope. Ain't nobody said what was missing. You ain't been around neither so how would you know that it was some pills and money missing unless you took 'em. Yeah, you guilty. I say let's mess up her face. That'll teach her you don't steal from fam."

Trish burst into tears. "I'm sorry, Shay! I'm so sorry! I don't know what's wrong with me. It's like I can't even control it. I just want to be high all the time, so I ain't got to feel nothing. I'm sorry, Shay."

Shay looked like she was going to accept Trish's apology for a moment, then her face hardened. She said, "I don't wanna hear that. You fu as hell stealing from fam! You thought you did something? It's plenty more where that came from. I was gone help you get to the bag, too, but I'm glad you showed yo' true colors."

"Yeah, we ain't need no cluck on the team," Cat chimed in.

An older Black woman teacher walked out of the room next to Trish's locker and noticed the girls pressing Trish. "What are you girls doing? Let that girl go right now," she demanded.

Plena released Trish's collar and the moment Trish was free, she bolted down the hallway leaving her locker wide open.

"We were just playing with her," Shay said.

The stern teacher stood there with her arms folded.

"It certainly didn't look like you were playing with her, but since she ran off, we'll never know. Young ladies, I suggest that you all find a classroom and get in it."

"Ok, we will," Shay said. "C'mon, y'all."

The girls walked off leaving Trish's locker open. Cat looked back at the teacher and rolled her eyes, but Shay pulled her along.

"We should have gave it to her, too," Cat complained. "She failed me freshie year. Ugly self. That's why her husband left her stiff-wig-wearing butt."

Shay kept hold of her arm. "You about to get into it with a teacher and we got weed and pills on us? You gone have us under the jailhouse. We came up here to hustle and that's it. This chick talkin' 'bout whupping a teacher. C'mon, Ronda Rousey. Remember the plan, go to class, let people know we got it and how they can get it. Forget Trish, we can catch her any time. I'll see y'all later, I'm going to the lunchroom."

Clutching her purse, Shay headed for the cafeteria, while Plena and Cat went their separate ways to their respective classes.

••••

On the first floor of the school, Trish burst into the security office. "Officer Swinson! Officer Swinson! They just tried to jump me on the second floor by my locker!"

Several male students were in the office showing Officer Swinson, the security head officer, a video on their cell phone. He was caught off guard, but he quickly recovered and sent the boys packing. "Alright, enough. Y'all get to class. Right now. Let's go."

Once the room was cleared, Officer Swinson looked at Trish. "What seems to be the problem, young lady?"

"Shay, I mean Shaniece Hampton and her friends are trying to jump me."

Disinterested, Officer Swinson fiddled with the computer on his desk. "Yeah? They trying to jump you, huh? Shaniece Hampton. Did they actually jump you or are they trying to jump you?"

"What? What difference do that make?' Trish asked with plenty of attitude. "They tried, that's all that matters. If it wasn't for that teacher who class by my locker then they would have did it. They threatened a CPS student on CPS property, I know for a fact that's a crime. Do I got to go to the principal and tell her you won't do nothin'?"

Officer Swinson stopped typing on the computer keyboard. "What's this girl's name, again?"

"Shaniece Hampton, but everybody call her Shay."

Officer Swinson perked up. "Shay? You said Shay? Now what's she trying to do to you?"

Trish folded her arms and rolled her eyes. She huffed, "I told you mall cop, Shaniece, Plena and Catrice were trying to jump me."

"For what?" Officer Swinson asked. "Y'all was girls, what happened? Better yet, what did you do?

"It's Shay! She be… uhhh hatin' on me. She gone tell Plena and Catrice nem that I stole her drugs and money. She got drugs on her, too. Right now in her purse, at school. She got pills and weed!"

Officer Swinson sat forward in his chair. "You say she got drugs on her? Where is she now?"

"I don't know, do yo' job, Officer Swinson," Trish whined. "I don't feel safe. You got to do yo' job."

Officer Swinson held up his hand to silence Trish. He referred to his computer and in seconds he had Shay's information on the monitor in front of him. He picked up his walkie-talkie. "Officers I've got a 452. Offender's name is Shaniece Hampton. She's in the cafeteria. Bring her to the security office. I repeat a 452. Copy?"

Several static filled responses of "copy" came through the radio. Officer Swinson looked at Trish. "Okay, young lady, we've got a hand on this. You can go to class."

Trish asked, "What about the rest of them?"

"They won't be a problem," Officer Swinson said confidently. "I'm personally going to make sure of that. Once we have the ringleader, we won't hear a peep out of the other culprits or they're going to jail, too."

The radio crackled to life. A security officer announced, "We've got her in custody. Bringing her to the office now."

"Copy that," Officer Swinson said into the walkie-talkie. To Trish, he said, "I told you, she's the ringleader. I'm going to nip this in the bud. Go ahead to class, Trina."

"Trish."

"Hunh?"

"My name is Trish, not Trina."

"That's what I said," Officer Swinson said impatiently. "Don't worry, I'll get it right in the report. Go to class." Trish peeked out the office door, looked both ways, there was no sign of her enemies, so she made her escape. Glad that she was finally gone, Officer Swinson pulled a hairbrush out of his desk and gave his wavy hair a quick brush. He took a small mirror out of his desk drawer and used it to check his teeth. He put the mirror back and had just enough time to slide a stick of gum in his mouth before two of his security officers opened the door and shoved a handcuffed, angry Shay into his office.

"What y'all grab me for, top flight?" she seethed. Officer Swinson came from behind his desk and took Shay by the arm. He steered her into a chair and shook hands with both officers. One officer sat Shay's purse on the desk.

"Thank you, thank you," Officer Swinson said graciously. "Good job, guys. Better get back to the cafeteria."

Officer Swinson closed and locked his office door behind the officers when they left. He retook his seat behind the desk and opened Shay's purse.

"You can't do that!" Shay shouted. "You can't search my purse!"

Officer Swinson continued searching her purse as he said with a smile, "Of course I can. I'm not a CPS employee, I'm CPD and I've got reason to believe you've got contraband and/or weapons in said purse. Well, lookie, lookie!" Officer Swinson pulled several bundles of weed and pills out of her purse. "Tisk, tisk, tisk. I hope that you know possession of a controlled substance with intent to deliver on CPS property, even the weed is a Class X felony, that's non-probationable.

Wow, Shay, you looking at some real time here. Let me call for transport."

All the fire was gone out of Shay as she hung her head. At least I left my burner in Cat car, she thought as she prepared herself to go to jail.

Officer Swinson paused before calling on his CPD radio. "Shay me and you always got along, right?"

Shay looked up at Officer Swinson, she saw something in his face, but she wasn't sure what it was. She decided to see where he was going with this line of questioning. "I thought we was cool, Swinson. I guess I thought wrong if you finta book me."

Officer Swinson left his seat and came around his desk to sit on its edge in front of Shay. "I know what's going on with your brothers right now. It's not a good time for you to be going to jail, is it? This is nothing compared to what they got going on. I don't want to see you go to jail, Shay. Matter of fact, I would hate to see you get locked up. I can help you if you help me."

"I ain't nobody's snitch," Shay said, shaking her head. "I don't know nothin' about what my brothers did or didn't do and nobody else."

Officer Swinson laughed. "That's wassup. You sound harder than most of these dudes I run into. They would have came through the door telling on any and everybody. But really, it's nothing like that, you help me and I can help you. I just need you to do something that you already do and all of this goes away."

"What's that?" Shay asked suspiciously. "What I gotta do to make all this go away?"

Officer Swinson leaned forward. "All I'm going to

say is, I saw your video. I just want you to treat me special like you did that boy in it."

Shay couldn't believe her luck. She laughed. "Is that all? And you gonna forget about everything that was in my purse?"

Officer Swinson unzipped his pants. "What purse? Who are you?"

Take these cuffs off and I got you," she said seductively.

Officer Swinson whipped out his keys. He was so excited that he fumbled around for a second, but he was eventually able to unlock the handcuffs. He dropped his pants to his ankles, sat on the edge of the desk and leaned back with his eyes closed.

"You ready?" she asked. "More than ready," Officer Swinson said, his voice trembling in anticipation. "Go head, I'm way past ready."

Shay gathered up all the force she could muster and gave him a stiff uppercut in his package. Officer Swinson fell off the desk and folded up in a fetal position on the floor, holding his wounded groin. Shay stood up, stepped over him and politely collected her drugs, which she stuffed back in her purse. She stepped over Officer Swinson again just as he began to vomit.

"Man, Swinson what you have for lunch?" Shay quipped as she was extra careful not to get any vomit on her shoes as she made it over to the door. She unlocked the door, peeked out and left, shutting the door behind her. Taking care to avoid any security guards, she exited the first door she came across without a chain.

Hurriedly Shay walked several blocks in record time. She ducked into a Subway sandwich shop on Cottage Grove and ordered a tuna sandwich. Once her sandwich was decked out with all the fixings, she took a seat. In between taking bites of her sandwich she checked her inboxes, texts, and DM. The word of her product had gotten around because she had plenty of messages. Most of them she'd missed coming in because she had turned her phone off in school so the teachers or security didn't try to confiscate it. If they did, you had to get your parents to come up to the school and get it back. The chances of Pat making a trip up to the school to get her phone back was slim to none, that's why she just turned it off.

She wouldn't have to worry about that anymore, though. Besides the fact that she'd just assaulted the school's head security officer, who just so happened to be a Chicago Police officer, she couldn't let school get in the way of her bread no more. As simple as that, she dropped out of school while checking her messages and eating a tuna sub. Unknowingly, she was following in the footsteps of her older sister and mother.

Shay sent Cat and Plena a text message, alerting them that they had police trouble and she'd left school. Cat replied they were on their way. Cat was taking forever, so Shay went into the liquor store and copped some Backwoods. She sat on the bus stop and rolled her wood like it was legal. Several customers called and texted while she was waiting and she told them she was on her way.

She was on her cell phone and smoking a blunt when Cat finally pulled up with Plena in the passenger's seat. Without ceremony she got in the back seat and Cat pulled off.

Cat and Plena started to talk, but Shay waved them off. "What took y'all so long? Y'all got us missing money."

Plena looked back over the seat at Shay. "Shay, we gotta tell you something."

"For real, for real, if it ain't about this bread, I don't want to hear it right now. I don't care what it is. This bread comes first. Let's bust these moves first then we can talk about whatever. Cat, swing a left up here, go to the middle of the block, it's a gray house. Plena gimme my gun out the armrest."

Plena's eyes widened. "What you need yo gun for, Shay? What you about to do?"

"I ain't finta do nothing, stop being so scary. I'm finta serve homie and I wanna make sure he see that we be having bangers and it ain't sweet."

To the customer Shay texted: Come down, I'm pulling up

The moment the car came to a stop, Shay poured out two ounces of lean into a baby bottle and tightened the cap. The door to the gray house opened and a young, shirtless guy covered in tattoos skipped down the steps and over to the car. When he leaned down to the back window, the first thing he noticed was the gun on Shay's lap.

He backed up quickly and said, "That's what y'all on? Y'all robbing the customers?"

"Nah, boy, stop actin' slow," Shay said harshly. "We hustlin', but we keep poles. Come on, get this so I can get off this hot block."

The boy threw caution to the winds and walked back close to the car. He handed Shay his money and she handed him his baby bottle. He held it up to the sunlight and squinted at it.

"It look like straight drop," he said. "If it is, you gone get off because ain't nobody got no lean. Once I taste it, I'll post it and they gone be hitting yo' line, shorty. A-ight now."

The boy jogged back to his house and they pulled off. For the next hour or so, Cat drove, while Shay served and Plena kept track of the cash. Eventually, the phone went dry for a moment and Shay decided it was time to clear the air.

Shay rolled another Backwood and lit it. "Now," she said, "what took y'all so long to pull up? I almost got bagged and then when I get up out that jam, I can't even count on y'all to scoop me. That's crazy."

"Girl, we had to sneak outta school," Cat explained. "When they told us that security grabbed you, we thought you was going to jail. We ain't know what to do so we went to the studio. We ain't know you was gone get out that jam. That's when…

Cat fell silent. She looked in the rear view mirror at Shay's face, then over at Plena.

"I'm just gone tell her," Plena said. "She gone find out anway. Shay we went to the studio after we left school, that's when we found out that Ace and Swan is dead."

"What? What did you say?"

In quieter tones, Plena repeated, "Ace and Swan is both dead. The twins killed them, we think for posting that video of you. They robbed them and shot them up."

"How y'all just gone say my brothers did that?!?" Shay shouted.

"Don't holler at me, Shay," Plena said. "Swan's grandmother saw the whole thing. One of the twins shot at her, too. I think that's them damn pills or Scottie that got them off the chain like that."

"What you say?"

"Shay, I don't know why you is actin' like that. I said I think them pills be havin' them lit like that. It gotta be somethin', they been shootin' peoples left and right. They trippin'!"

"It sound like you tryna accuse me or something. It's like you sayin' because I gave them the pills it's my fault? Or that I told them to do that because Swan put that video up of me?"

Plena looked at Shay with pure amazement. "Girl, you is trippin'! Like for real, for real. I don't know what's wrong with you, but I didn't say that. What is you hearin'?"

"You might not have said it, but you meant it Plena. I know you, I can tell you wanna say that. I ain't tell them to do nothin'."

"What the hell is wrong with you?" Plena aked. "You must be 'noid off all that weed you smokin' girl. Ain't nobody said that you told them to kill Ace and Swan. They is already some bugs and I don't think givin' them pills help with that, but it ain't yo fault."

"I knew it!" Shay shouted. "That is what you think! Pull over right now Cat! Right now, dammit! I'd rather walk than ride with two fake friends. I ain't playing Cat, let me out right now!"

"Girl, you is doing too much," Cat said as she looked for a safe place to pull out of traffic.

Shay got out of the car, slammed the car door and took a seat on the curb.

Plena got out of the car and stood over Shay. "Shay, really? Really? This how you finta do? You act like we against you, we always been with you. Come on get in the car, we outta here."

Shay lit a cigarette and sat back. "I'm not playin'. I don't need people around me that be sneak-dissin'. I can't trust y'all. I'm finta get up with my brothers and find out what's goin' on, while y'all goin' around tellin' everybody I told the twins to kill Ace. Don't nobody know for sure if they did that, but y'all be quick to repeat a rumor. Y'all can gone 'bout y'all business."

Plena saw there was no reasoning with Shay, so she got back in the car. Cat had had her fill of Shay's tantrum and she drove away without a word. Shay sat on the curb, smoking her cigarette and trying to call her family, but no one answered. She didn't know what else to do, so she pulled up her social media sites on her phone, hoping it was just a rumor that Ace was dead; it wasn't. When she went on Ace's page, his wall was already flooded with Rest In Peace wishes and condolences.

As she scrolled through the comments, tears streamed down her face. Soon she was openly wailing.

She forgot about her new clothes and her Gucci bag full of drugs, money and a gun. Shay put her head in her lap and cried her eyes out while she sat on the curb.

CHAPTER 21__

Nayshawn and Jayshawn sat on a minivan's discarded rear seat on the back porch of an ancient house across the street from the park. They passed a dipped blunt between the both of them. Nayshawn hit the blunt and stood up. He pulled out his pistol.

"Bro, I love the way Scottie make me feel, bro," Nayshawn said while aiming his gun at imaginary targets. "On Snipes, I be feelin' so good I can't even describe it, bro. It's like you can see and taste the air. It's like you be ready for anything, but ain't nothing movin' too fast for you. Not on no corny white boy from the Matrix type stuff, neither. Everything is going at the speed you want it to, especially when you clappin' at somebody. It's like you can't miss. You see how I hit that sucker that posted Shay, bro?"

Jayshawn rested his head on the headrest of the minivan seat. "You did him dirty, twin. I love you for that, bro! You did that how you was 'sposed to do it. I was like, yeah. It was like, I was watching a movie."

"Bro, I'm ready for some action now! I ain't finta be hiding bro, that's for lames.

We shole can't live in no backyard or garages, and now the big homie Treadwell won't answer the door. We know you in there, you on house arrest. On Snipes bro, we can't go nowhere near the crib and you already know Pat's house on fire, bro."

"On God," Jayshawn agreed. "We too hot, bro. On Snipes, I really ain't too mad that we can't go to the crib. I don't wanna go there no way. I know Pat trippin' and Shay probably cappin' over that lame of hers we wet up."

Nayshawn squinted with one eye and aimed at a bird on the ground. He said, "He shouldn'ta been playin' with our sister and being disrespectful. Bro, seriously though, I'm thinkin' we should get up outta here for a minute. Maybe we can holla at Dee."

"Boy, Dee way to bougie, she don't mess with us. We need to rob her lame baby daddy. Want this last hit, bro?"

Nayshawn put his gun away and sat down, his leg wouldn't stop moving. "Nall bro, we ain't got time for that. I'm thinking we should take somebody car and get little. We can link up with bro and nem in Minnesota. Plus, we got family in the Sota Pop."

"On Snipes, remember that fat white chick that go with our cuzzo Eric that live up there? Remember when they came to visit for his mama funeral and she made that caramel cake? On God, that was the best cake I ever had in my life. I want some of that cake right now, Nay! On everything I love."

Jayshawn stood up. "Bro, well that's where we going. We just gotta get us a car and then we on the road, headed to go get us some of that caramel cake. Let's go, twin. I can taste that cake now. Plus, we can't sit around here 'til we get popped off. If we make it to Minnesota, we can chill and won't nobody know where we went."

The twins left the backyard and walked down the alley.

"It's simple, twin," Jayshawn said as they walked amongst the debris in the trash strewn alley. "We go up here to the gas station, chill for minute, wait 'til we see somebody leave they car running and we out with it. We got GPS on our phones, too. Long as the car decent, we gone make it. What you think, twin?"

"Let's go," Nayshawn said.

The walk to the gas station was a short one and soon the twins were loitering by the gas pumps looking for a victim. Several vehicles drove in and out of the station, but they didn't meet the twins' specifications so they let them go. Nayshawn and Jayshawn were unaware that inside the gas station store, the clerk noticed their shady looks and placed a call to police about suspicious persons on the premises.

Nayshawn walked away from the gas pumps and over to the mini store. He opened the door of the gas station store for customers, while keeping an eye out for any customer that left their car running. Jayshawn stayed over by one of the gas station pumps. Nothing was looking promising until a young woman pulled into the gas station in a late model Lexus SUV. She parked by a pump and got out. She left the truck running as she went into the mini market. Jayshawn signaled to Nayshawn as he climbed into the SUV. Nayshawn peeked through the store door and saw the SUV's owner was in the lottery line. He skipped over to the Lexus truck and got into the passenger seat. As Jayshawn drove to the exit and prepared to enter traffic, the SUV owner ran out of the gas station store building. The woman ran up to the SUV and began banging on the window.

"Get out of my truck!" she yelled. "You're not taking my truck! Get out of my truck you thieving bastard! Give me back my car!"

Nayshawn held up his gun and pointed it at the woman. Stunned, she backed off. On the other end of the gas station, a Chicago Police cruiser entered the gas station lot. The SUV owner spotted the cop car and ran over to it.

While she ran, she shouted, "Stop them they're stealing my car! Police! Police! They're stealing my truck! They got a gun! Stop them!"

The blue and white police car stopped by the frantic woman.

"What happened?" the policeman asked from the passenger seat. "What happened, miss?"

The woman pointed frantically at her SUV as it merged into traffic. "That's my car, they just took it when I went in the store! It's two of them and one of them pointed a gun at me!"

The policeman burned rubber as he peeled off in pursuit. He turned on his siren as he grabbed his radio and called for backup. Lights flashing, the police cruiser caught up to Jayshawn two blocks away. The police car attempted to pull over the SUV, but instead of stopping, Jayshawn gunned the engine and sped off. The police car gave chase.

Jayshawn gripped the steering wheel tightly as he sped west on 79th to King Drive. He barely missed running over a small crowd of dopefiends crossing the street. He sent them sprawling in the street as he slid around the corner. The SUV grazed a CTA bus as Jayshawn straightened the vehicle and flew north on King Drive.

"I'm finta get this blue and white up off us," Nayshawn said as he let the window down. He hung halfway out the window and emptied his gun at the pursuing police car. The police car swerved, but continued to chase them. As they blew through the intersection at 76th and King Drive, two more blue and whites joined the chase.

Nayshawn hurriedly reloaded his gun and leaned out the window again to bang at the cops.

"Get in here, boy!" Jayshawn yelled. "It's too many of them now. Hold on, bro, I'm finta try and make it to the e-way."

On 75th Street, Jayshawn swung a hard left and rocketed westward in the direction of the Dan Ryan expressway. 75th Street was crowded and Jayshawn had to slow down as he weaved his way through cars and pedestrians. He honked the SUV's horn furiously as he drove on the wrong side of the two-way street. Cars moved to the side and people dove out of his way and soon he was past the mini traffic jam.

At the corner of 75th and Michigan the police had set up a roadblock with several of their cars. Jayshawn recognized the road block and smashed through it anyway. Most of the officers dove out of the way, but two officers stood their ground and emptied their weapons at the truck as it went through the roadblock.

At the officers' fire, both twins got down and popped up half a block later. Jayshawn continued on to the expressway and swung a right on State Street. The expressway entrance ramp was blocked by two State police.

"Damn!" Jayshawn bellowed. "They is everywhere, bro!"

"On God," Nayshawn said, his voice shaking slightly from fear. "What we gone do, bro?"

"Watch this, bro," Jayshawn said with way more confidence than he felt. "Like GTA, boy." He swung a totally unexpected u-turn, catching the pursuing police vehicles off-guard, and all they could do was move to the side to avoid a head-on collision with the SUV. Jayshawn barreled up State Street the wrong way for two blocks before he had to avoid two trucks, so he swung left at 77th and State Street. He overshot the turn and sideswiped a pickup truck. He backed up out of the side of the pickup, straightened up and picked up speed again. They managed to make it several blocks before a tire blew out without warning and Jayshawn crashed into the back of a minivan and the SUV cut off. He tried to restart it, but it wouldn't catch, so they got out of the totaled vehicle and ran.

Police cars screeched to a halt almost as soon as the twins cleared the stolen Lexus SUV. As they ran, Nayshawn pointed his pistol at the police. He managed to get off a couple of shots before they made it through the driveway, on the side of someone's house, as they headed for the backyard. Several policemen returned fire striking him in the back. He staggered into the backyard where Jayshawn was about to jump the fence to enter the next yard.

"Aaaawww! I'm hit!" Nayshawn screamed as he fell onto the soft grass of the backyard. "Jay, I'm hit! I'm hit!"

Jayshawn climbed down off the fence and rushed over to his brother. "Where, bro? I can't see no holes. You sure? C'mon bro, we gotta get up outta here. Let's go, bro! You sure you hit?"

"In my back, they hit me in my back."
Jayshawn tried to help Nayshawn to his feet, but his brother couldn't get up.

"Please, get up, bro," Jayshawn begged. "Please, bro, I need you to get to this fence, I ain't gone leave without you, so I need you to get up, bro."

In response, Nayshawn dropped his gun.

"Get up, twin, we gotta go! Come on, twin!" Jayshawn pleaded. "Jay, don't give up on me. What's wrong with you? I can't even see where you hit. Twin, let's go, bro!"

As he lay on the grass, Nayshawn wasn't saying anything anymore. He was sweating profusely and couldn't seem to catch his breath. Jayshawn noticed that his brother's blood has begun to stain the grass. Gently, he turned him over and saw five bullet holes in Nayshawn's back. Blood was pouring from them.

"Nay!" Jayshawn yelled. "Bro, we still got to get up out of here. If you can't move, I got to go get you some help. I gotta go, Nay. I can't stay here or we're both caught, bro. I won't forget about you bro, I'll send you some help."

Nayshawn started sobbing. He wheezed, "Don't leave me, bro. Please don't leave me. I can't really breathe, bro and I'm cold. Please don't leave me, twin. Jay where are you?"

Jayshawn started crying. "I'm right here, I ain't gone leave you like this, Nay. I ain't going nowhere, bro. I'm right here, twin."

"Jay, I'm so cold, twin. So cold. Where are you? I can't see you Jay. Don't leave me by myself twin. Please don't leave me, bro."

"I'm right here, twin," Jayshawn said as he sobbed wildly. He grasped his twin's hand which was ice cold and slick with his blood. "I'm right here Nay, I ain't going nowhere. I'm…"

Policemen flooded the backyard and pointed their guns at the twins. They shouted, "Get your hands up! Don't move!"

Jayshawn raised his hands. "Help my brother! He's shot! He's hurt real bad! Call the ambulance!"
The policemen rushed over and tackled the brothers. They flipped them over to handcuff them both while they were lying on their stomachs. As they lay side by side, Jayshawn looked over at his brother.

"Hang in there, Nay," he sobbed. "They gotta take you to the hospital. Just hold on, bro. Can you hear me?"

In response, Nayshawn coughed a huge glob of blood onto the ground and closed his eyes for the last time.

Jayshawn hollered, "Nnnnnoooooo! Please help him! Help him! Help my bro! Don't let him die like this! Help him!"

"Shut up before you join him," a large Black officer growled. He kicked Jayshawn as hard as he could in the ribs. The kick knocked the wind out of him. When he could breathe again, he sobbed quietly. His tears were for his twin because he knew no help was coming. He also knew his twin's death would haunt him for many nightmare filled nights to come.

CHAPTER 22

Pat's friend, Rhonda pulled into the parking space down the street from the Odyssey Lounge on Garfield. She looked over at Pat after she put the car in park. Pat was busy in the passenger seat checking her hair in the sun visor mirror.

"Pat," she said softly. "You gone be alright, heffa? You sure want to be goin' out so soon after what just happened to the twins?"

Pat never stopped fixing her hair as she answered, "Girl, don't get to boohooin' for them little murderous bastards. I don't feel like it no mo'. Crying is for funerals. They both where tears ain't gone help them, like my granny used to say."

"Damn, I know you heartless Pat, but them is yo' kids."

"You think I don't know that?!" Pat exploded. "You think my heart ain't broke right now? Those was my twin boys, my babies! What can I do, though? Sittin' around being all sad ain't gonna make it no better. Do you know how crazy it is for newspaper reporters to be running up trying to ask me questions? Do you know how it feel to have one son dead, and the other charged with five murders, plus about 12 attempt murders on the police? How could I not care about that? I'm not the devil, but I do want me a drink, and to socialize, so I can get this off my mind for maybe a minute or two."

"You so strong though, Pat. If this was my sons, I would be in Tinley Park, because I would straight up lose my mind. How is you holdin' together?"

Pat flipped the sun visor close and lit a cigarette. She inhaled and blew the smoke out into the chilly night air. "I don't even know. I guess I'm just prepared. My mama, my uncles nem, and my cousins has been in mess like this my whole life. Someone was always shooting somebody, or dying, or getting locked up. The twins' daddy was a killer until he got killed. Shay and Dee daddy probably got 50 more years to do in the joint. I prayed to Jesus, God and Allah that they would be different. I bought them everything they could want growing up... $200 shoes, expensive clothes and video games. I see none of that mattered because look where they are now. I had insurance on them, so once they release Nay's body, I'm gone put my baby away in style. I'll save my tears for that day because like I said life goes on, with or without you."

"Well, I'll drink to that," Rhonda said and pulled a huge flask out of her purse. "I know you wanna party and keep yo' mind off things, so we ain't gotta talk about it no mo'. If you need to talk though, don't hesitate to say something, and I mean that Pat. The Odyssey yo' spot hunh, Pat? Do yo' guy Luther know yo' sneaky butt up here?"

Pat began applying fresh eye liner around her eyes. "What Luther don't know you could fill up Soldier's Field with, but that's neither here nor there, because what he don't know can't hurt him. His fat butt at home with his fat wife anyway. I ain't been accepting his calls for a few days and he goin' crazy! Now, he promisin' to leave his big back wife for me. I told him to call me back when he got a crib of his own, and his signature is on the divorce papers."

"Pat you is heartless. Why you doing that to that man? I kinda like Luther. That man is nice and he treat you like a queen."

"Girl, I don't want to talk about him no more," Pat said irritably. "Gimme that bottle, I'm trying to get drunk."

Rhonda started to curse Pat out for snapping at her, but she kept her cool. She took a healthy swig from her flask and handed it to Pat, while rolling her eyes. After a few minutes, the tension in the car subsided. Rhonda turned the radio on and they sipped vodka, talked, joked and laughed for another ten minutes before going into the lounge. Inside, they found some seats and ordered some beers.

CHAPTER 23

Dee was standing at the kitchen sink sipping from a glass of wine and lost deep in thought. She fingered the packet of pills in her pocket for the thousandth time. In the week since she'd returned, she looked for any sign of change in Que's behavior, but there hadn't been any. It was almost like she'd never overheard that diabolical conversation. She had made an excuse for the last couple of days to sleep on the couch, in Honey's room or on the chaise lounge. No amount of sheet changing or Lysol spraying would let her sleep in that bed ever again.

Things weren't great, but they weren't bad enough to slip him a mickey she thought. She had pretty much chickened out on doing that to him, but a couple of things happened in a span of less than 72 hours to change that. The first thing was she checked his secret Instagram page from one of her various fake pages. Under several of his posts, he bragged that he was on his way to Houston, to take over, and show them how to get money real soon.

A few days ago, she'd received the bad news about her younger twin brothers. When she turned to Que for comfort, he was quite nasty when he said, 'they got what they deserve, they shoulda been gettin' some money instead of wildin' out'. She was heartbroken by his response and didn't speak to him for two whole days. He actually seemed to enjoy her silence.

The third thing had just happened a few moments ago. Que told her he had to make a run and he came back with several gifts for her, a new large Louis Vuitton duffle bag, several pairs of shoes, and a tennis bracelet. When she asked what all the stuff was for, he said to celebrate that he was letting her go on her own to Wyoming to bust a few moves, and she would be there for a while. He gave some sappy speech about how it was her time and he was putting her on. He told her that she could keep everything for herself. Dee's heart started beating fast because she knew this was it; this was the way he would get rid of her. In the back of her mind, she had tried to fool herself that maybe things would work out. After all she was his child's mother, he couldn't be heartless enough to get her locked away while he moved on with their child and his side chick. Obviously, he was though. She couldn't deny it, Que was smooth. If she didn't have prior knowledge of his scheme she would have fell for it hook, line, and sinker.

Forget it, she thought, if he don't get me now, he still gone get me. I can't be watching over my back everyday from the person closest to me.

Dee shook one of the pills into her palm and put the other one into her jogging pants pocket. She cuffed the first pill in between her index and middle finger. She picked up her wine glass with the hidden pill hand and went back to the living room. Que was in his favorite place on the couch wearing his basketball shorts and a tank top, sipping from his usual double cup of lean while he smoked a blunt. Dee put her wine glass down on the coffee table and took Que's double cup from him and placed it on the coffee table, too. She was careful to let the pill tumble from between her fingers into his lean as she did.

She thought he would protest, but instead he welcomed her as she climbed onto his lap. He wrapped his arms around her, something he hadn't done in a long time. As she smelled his cologne, a million of their memories leapt in her mind. She was almost ready to knock over the tainted cup of lean, when he put his lips next to her ear. He whispered hoarsely, "I think you should probably spend tomorrow with Honey because you might not be seeing her in awhile. You know on account of you being out of town."

Dee's heart fell down into her stomach at his words. She climbed off of his lap and readjusted her clothes.

"What?" Que asked. "Baby what happened?"

"It's nothing, here you go, baby," Dee replied as she handed him the cup of lean. She peeked in the cup as she passed it to him, the pill had totally dissolved. "I just started getting a charley horse. I'll be right back, I'm going to get some more wine."

Que drained the half cup of the spiked lean and poured himself some more. "Don't take too long, girl."

Dee took her time in the kitchen. She opened the refrigerator and was about to pour herself another glass of wine, when she decided against it, and selected a fresh bottle of Moet Rose` she'd been saving for a special occasion. She sat the bottle on the countertop and opened it, taking care not to pop the cork and get rose` everywhere. She selected a gold-rimmed champagne glass from the shelf and poured herself a glass. She carried the bottle and sipped from her champagne flute as she went back into the living room.

Quincy was sitting in the same place she'd left him. A little blood had trickled out of the corner of his mouth and out of one nostril. His head lolled back on the couch and he seemed barely unconscious, but he still held his double cup. Dee sat on the couch beside him and observed him for a while. As he made gurgling noises and flopped his head around, she knew the pill had done its job.

Dee poured herself another glass of champagne and toasted him. "I hope you can hear me, you piece of dirt. I'm gone take Honey and raise her well away from you. Nobody in your family will ever see her or hear from her again. Don't worry though, you'll get your chance to go home to your momma, she ruined you anyway. Pat warned me about you over and over again, but I wouldn't listen. You stole my youth and my family life away from me. I can't believe I actually thought that you loved me." She paused to drain her champagne flute. "I knew you had other women, but to see it with my own two eyes in the bed where I sleep. Wow! Not only that, you were plotting to get me locked up. Me! I'm the only person keeping it 100 out of everybody and you want to get me locked up? Me? I can't even look at you no more."

Dee put her cup down and picked up the designer

duffle bag. She took it in the bedroom where she sat it on the bed so she could pull on a t-shirt and the jacket to her jogging suit. She slipped on a pair of running shoes and pulled her hair into a ponytail. She went to the closet and took down four shoeboxes filled with cash from the shelves there. She dumped the cash into the duffle bag.

Next, she went to Honey's room and moved her daughter's chest of drawers out of the corner. She peeled back the carpet there and revealed Que's stash of cash. He'd actually thought that he was hiding it from her. She put that money into the Louis Vuitton bag as well. She removed the last mickey pill from her pocket and put it in the inside pocket and zipped the bag up. She went to get her car keys. Quietly, she let herself out of the apartment and made her way to the building's parking garage. She deposited the bag in her trunk and went back upstairs to the apartment.

Que was sitting in the same exact spot on the couch, he was still gurgling like a baby and he had peed himself. Dee sat on the coffee table directly in front of him. She poured herself another glass of champagne and touched it to the double Styrofoam cup Que was still clutching in a mock toast.

"Now, where were we?" Dee said. "Oh, I know. What I really hate is I let you steal my youth. When I met you, yo' grown ass ain't have no business talkin' to a girl my age. But, what I came to realize is that even though you were grown. I was about your speed. You taught me so much. You never have to worry about me loving anybody else, baby daddy. You ruined it for everybody. Thank you though for the lessons and the blessings, Honey and me are super-straight."

With one huge gulp she finished off her glass of champagne. The bubbles made her giggle a little as she leaned over and whispered in Quincy's ear. She whispered, "Not you or yo' fat mama will never see Honey again. I'll make sure that she forgets about you, too. She'll never know what happened to her snake of a father and you'll never know what happened to her. Goodbye, bae."

She kissed Que on the forehead and took care to wipe any traces of her kiss off of his face. She picked up the house phone and dialed 911 and waited for the call to be picked up.

"Help me!" she yelled into the phone the second it connected. "It's my boyfriend, he's taken something and he not actin' right. Yes, it was drugs, he drinks lean and pops pills everyday! Please hurry, I don't know what to do! Yes, I think he did have a seizure. Help him please, I can't live without him. I love bae!"

She had to hold the phone away from her face because she couldn't help but snicker at her performance. She got back on the phone. "Yes, I'm here. You can get the address from the phone. Okay, help is on the way, alright. Thank you, thank you."

Dee poured herself some more champagne and resigned herself to waiting for the paramedics. She knew she would have to play the concerned girlfriend role for a while longer, but soon it would be over.

CHAPTER 24

Shay looked around her motel room. She'd been chilling there for the last five days getting as high as possible. She hadn't answered her cell phone since she'd been here and she kept her gun close, even going to the bathroom with it.

She thought having money would make her feel better, but it didn't. She was feeling guilty and terrible about her little brothers. Killing Ace and Swan. Finding out about Nay being killed. Jay getting locked up via the internet. She drank, smoked, and cried for days about them.

All it took was for her to call Pat blubbering and Pat sat her straight quickly, but with the truth. She said they knew what they was doing. What did they think was going to happen if they kept killing people? Pat ended the conversation by telling her she wasn't grown yet and she needed to come home. She had to admit when she hung up she wasn't feeling as bad.

She decided, the first thing she needed to do was reconnect with her friends. She hadn't talked to her squad since the day she'd gotten out of Cat's car. It had taken a couple of days, but realized they hadn't done anything wrong, so she decided to reach out.

She sent Plena a text: Where y'all at

Plena: On the studio block

Shay: Finta slide

Shay called an Uber and in six minutes she was on the way to the block. On the block, plenty of partygoers were milling around drinking and getting high as they mourned Ace and Swan. Shay got out of the Uber car and began to look around for her friends. The crowd started to notice Shay and a couple of Swan and Ace's friends gave her hateful looks. Shay spotted Plena and Cat sitting on the trunk of Cat's car and she made her way over to them.

Shay tried to greet her friends like nothing had transpired between them. "What's poppin', y'all? I'm sorry I was…"

Plena held up her hand. "Save it, Shay, we straight. I know you was goin' through some stuff, but if you stunt like that again, you gone catch these hands."

"You ain't the only one with hands, Plena!" Shay stated. "But like I was sayin', I'm sorry. I know y'all gang all day. I was tweakin'."

"Well, you tweakin' now comin' through here," Cat said. "Shay, you need to get from up off the block. Yo' little brothers killed they guys. These boys is big mad about that. You need to get up out of here!"

Shay looked around and put her hand in her purse. "Can't nobody make me go nowhere, I'm from the block. They better fall back."

Shay noticed all the hate-filled looks she was getting. Things had definitely changed since the last time she was here.

Plena kept looking around as she said, "Look girl, forget all that. Believe me when I tell you that you got to put some space between you and this place. These Negroes is ready to trip. They talking real foxy 'bout what they gone do to you. You need to go that a-way, right away. I'll hit yo line."

"They on it like that with me?" Shay asked with a bit of fear in her voice.

"On sight," Cat said urgently. "Some boys with some big guns walked through about 10 minutes ago talking crazy. Fern and them that used to be at the studio with us was actin' shady, but when the rest of them wasn't looking, Fern did slide on us. He told us to tell you to stay off the set and off the block and definitely off the Nine. I keep tellin' you, you need to move around, like right now."

Plena hugged Shay quickly. "Gone now, dip through that yard right there. Go!"

With nothing more to say, Shay pulled her gun out her purse and walked away. She cut through the first yard, ducked through a gangway, went down the set of stairs there and out to the alley. She cut through another gangway and was gone.

Five minutes hadn't passed after she left before two boys walked up to Cat and Plena. Both of the boys were carrying guns in their hands and had t-shirts wrapped around their faces. They peered at Plena and Cat closely. One boy headed toward them, but the other boy grabbed his arm.

" What, bro?" the boy asked, "Is that her, bro? Is that her?"

The other boy said, "That ain't her."

"On Swan, they said she was over here and that she

was tall. That broad right there is tall, bro, that gotta be her. I'm finta wack her. I know it ain't no two tall girls be out here."

The boy started toward Cat and Plena again, but his friend grabbed him again. "Nall boy, on Ace, I'm steady tellin' you that ain't her! Now you just gone shoot every girl that's tall in America? I know what she look like! She used to be in the studio with bro nem and that ain't her. That's why I walked over here with you because you don't know what she looks like, and you'll be done bodied a innocent chick for nothin'."

"Well, if that ain't her, I bet she know where she went. I'm finta ask her."

Still brandishing his gun, the boy walked up to Plena. "Aye, you know Shay? She was just out here. Which way she went?"

Plena played it cool and her voice wasn't challenging when she said, "She was out here for a minute, but she got up outta here. She said she was finta go up on the Nine and see what was poppin' up that way. Said she was finta get some Chinese food or somethin'."

The boy stared at Plena like he was trying to tell if she was lying or not. He didn't point his gun directly at her, but it wasn't really pointed away from her either.

"Your girl is foul," the boy said. "Let her know we on her heels. Let her know when we jump down on her ain't no talkin'. She had fool nem do my cuz dirty, that ain't never ridin'. Y'all better stay away from her too, because when we catch her, we ain't got no time to try and separate and figure out who is who. Remember I told you, 'cause ain't no second warning." To his friend, he said, "Come on, boy, she couldn't have got too far. I'm suddenly in the mood for some Chinese food."

The two boys ran off and Plena and Cat finally breathed again.

"Cat, you see that? They was ready to pull it. I hope Shay don't think it's sweet. These boys is not playin'! You know what, on bro and nem, we need to get up out of here before these dummies decide to kill us because they can't catch Shay."

Cat jumped down off of the car. "My thoughts exactly," she said.

CHAPTER 25

Detectives Farillo and Williams along with a police department psychologist knocked on Pat's apartment door. There was no immediate answer, so Detective Williams pounded on the door. That did the trick.

"I'm comin', dammit!" Pat yelled. "Stop beatin' on my door like you lost yo' damn mind!"

They heard footsteps followed by Pat yanking the door open. She looked at the police personnel standing in her hallway. "What? What y'all want?"

"Ma'am, does Nayshawn and Jayshawn Crawford live here?" Detective Farillo asked as he flashed his badge in Pat's face.

Pat blew smoke into his face from her ever present cigarette. She folded her arms across her chest. "I can't believe you actually asked do Nayshawn and Jayshawn live here. Well, let's see, Nayshawn don't live no where because you black hearted police kilt him. As for Jayshawn, he in y'all custody with no hope of bond or ever comin' home so you know where he at, too. What do y'all want or are y'all here to kill me too?"

"Well, there are two things," Detective Williams started.

"Get to the point man, I'm missing Love & Hip-Hop," Pat said with a bored look on her face.

"Well, the first thing is, this gentleman is a

department psychologist that specializes in grief counseling. The city has a new program that when a city employee causes the death of a citizen, the city offers the immediate family grief counseling if they want the service. At this time, is this something that you or anyone in your immediate family would like?"

"Do I look like I want counseling? I want my son back!" Pat snarled. "I know what y'all trying to do. Y'all trying to get on my good side so I won't sue the police department and this city. Well, y'all will hear from my lawyer because Black lives matter! Now, if there isn't anything else."

Pat moved to close her door, but Detective Williams stopped her. "There is just one more thing, Mrs. Crawford."

"I ain't no Crawford and the name is Pat."

"Okay, Pat," Det. Williams continued. "I know this may be hard for you, but we're going to need a statement from you."

"I ain't making no statement. What kind of statement do y'all need from me? What I'm 'sposed to say? Oh, I know, I got a dead kid and another one in jail. There's my statement."

"We can take you to the station and get your statement," Detective Farillo said impatiently.

"Let me get my purse," Pat said. "Let's go and believe me I'm gone do plenty of screamin' and cryin' about how y'all treatin' me and y'all kilt my child. Black lives matter!"

Pat and Farillo stared one another up and down. Williams stepped in and broke up their stare battle.

He handed Pat his card.

"Okay Pat, we apologize, we'll try again another day. We're sorry for your loss. And we're sorry to have bothered you."

The detectives and psychologist turned to leave, but Pat stopped them.

"When are they going to release his body?" she asked in softer tones. Her voice almost broke when she said, "I want to put him away and give his friends and family a chance to mourn."

Det. Farillo was about to answer, but Williams put his hand on Farillo's chest. He said, "His body should be released shortly, Pat. Any day now in fact. He was part of the investigation, but it's coming to a head. I'll call you personally the moment his body is released."

She looked at his business card. "Thank you, Detective Williams," she said with almost no attitude. "Let me know."

Pat closed her apartment door and went back to the living room to finish watching her program.

CHAPTER 26

A black Chevy Blazer pulled into the driveway alongside the brick bungalow home at 69th and Maplewood. The driver, a heavyset Black man with short dreadlocks placed a call, and in moments Patron exited the house. He was wearing all black clothes and carrying an all-black AK-47 pistol on a strap around his neck. He climbed into the Blazer and got comfortable with his gun on his lap.

"Pull off, Kevo" Patron ordered. "We can't sit right here with this heat."

"Patron, you my guy and all," Kevo said. "But, homie, this the fourth night in the last week that we been sliding through the set you think she from, and we still ain't seen hide nor hair of her."

"Boy, I wouldn't care if it was 800 days in a row," Patron said disgustedly. "You saw what they did to my face. You know what type of bread and the amount of product they took from me? They pistol-whipped me and took my jewelry. They was very disrespectful, bro. To top it all off, they threw my car keys down the block. You know this because when I got out the hospital, you had to go back there and help me find them. They did this to me because of her, and I'm going to find her and knock her noodles out. Ain't no talkin'. Now like I said, pull off."

Kevo shook his head, but he put the truck in reverse and backed out the driveway. "I'm just saying, bro, Chicago a big city. Ain't no tellin' where this chick could be at, bro."

"You worried about the wrong thing, Kevo. This is a hood chick, bro. Hood chicks don't leave they hood. If she do, she ain't goin' too far. She told me she from around 79th and Cottage and she was proud when she said that. She from off one of these blocks and that's where we gonna find her, on one of these blocks."

As Kevo steered the trunk in the direction of 79th Street, he asked, "Is you tryin' to trunk the broad and make her tell you who the robbers was?"

Again Patron looked at his friend. "Do I look like a kidnapper? Do you see me with rope or handcuffs or anything? All I got is a gun. She ain't gone give nobody up no way, it was probably her baby daddy or her guy. Girls like that have crazy loyalty. That would be a waste of time and could go real bad. We could end up in MCC fightin' a federal kidnappin' beef. Like I said, it would be a waste of time. Nall I ain't trunking her, I'm gone do her dirty to make sure she can't do that to nobody else."

"Makes sense," Kevo agreed as he turned east onto 79th Street. "Makes a lot of sense."

••••

Dee parked her car in front of Pat's apartment building just as her cell phone rang. She answered, "Hey, girl. Just coming from the grocery store. Yeah, you know ain't nothing in the fridge. Pat always sell her stamps. If Honey wasn't here, too I wouldn't even worry about it, but I don't want to get her started on that restaurant food. Between Pat and Shay, my baby would be orderin' Italian beefs and gyro fries."

Dee popped the trunk lid and got out the car. She was still on the phone as she walked around to the rear of the vehicle. "I'm only here for a minute. No, I ain't. Girl, I'm gone. Pat ain't finta get on my last nerve. I don't even want to hear it. You got me messed up, my bag decent, I ain't gotta stay here. I can do what I want to do, I'm only here for a minute. If it wasn't for the twins I wouldn't be here now. I think I'm headed for Cali or somewhere nice and warm. I'm sick of this crazy, violent city and it got the nerve to be cold. I'm going somewhere warm. Look, girl, call me later, I'm going to the party with you. Call me later, I got to carry these grocery bags."

Dee put her phone in her back pocket and started taking bags out the trunk. She looked at her duffel bag full of money, but decided against taking it into Pat's house. As she reached into the trunk for more bags, a black truck stopped in the street beside Dee's car.

The passenger in the black Blazer peered at Dee. She straightened up and looked at the passengers of the truck, but she didn't recognize them. As she stood there with several grocery bags on her arm, the passenger in the truck leaned out the car with his gun.

"What up, Shay," Patron said before he started to fire. She screamed as the bullets hit her and dropped her groceries as she fell between the two cars.

Patron got out of the truck leaving the door wide open. He stood over Dee and pumped more rounds into her chest. The extra rounds weren't necessary; she was already dead. He stopped firing and peered at his victim. Now that he took a closer look, he realized it wasn't Shay.

He turned back to Kevo in the truck. "Man this ain't even her! She look like her though, but it ain't her."

"Boy, would you bring yo' crazy butt on!" Kevo said urgently. "Come on, ain't nothing we can do about it now!"

" Damn, my bad baby girl," Patron said as he looked down at Dee and crossed himself. "Sorry about that. Wrong place at the wrong time, sometimes life is funny like that."

As Patron turned to get back into the truck, he noticed the Louis Vuitton duffel bag in the open trunk. He picked it up and inspected it. He held it up to Kevo.

"Man, this is real. This boy go crazy! I needs this!"

Patron took the designer bag, climbed into the truck and Kevo drove away leaving Dee's corpse surrounded by groceries. A broken half gallon leaked orange juice onto the asphalt which mingled with the blood escaping her body. As he tried to put as much distance as he could between them and Dee's dead body, Kevo kept looking over at Patron and shaking his head. Patron unzipped the bag and was shocked to find the bag full of money.

"Look at this, bro!" Patron exclaimed, as he held the bag so Kevo could see the contents.

"That's wassup!" Kevo commented. "We just came up."

"Nall, bro I just came up," Patron corrected him as

he searched the bag. "I'm gone hit you with something, though." He found the mickey pill in one of the bag's inner compartments. He held it up. "What have we here? I could use a turn up, too."

As Kevo saw Patron preparing to pop the pill he'd just found, Kevo asked, "Do you think that's wise my dude? You about to pop a pill you just found in a bag full of money."

"That's how I know it's alright," Patron said before placing the pill on his tongue. "My luck is changing, bro. I can't lose."

CHAPTER 27

Shay sat at the kitchen table with Honey eating cereal. Pat came into the kitchen and took a seat at the table with them. She moved the half gallon of milk out of the way and poured herself a shot from the Hennessy bottle on the table. She sat back and lit her customary cigarette.

Honey spooned cereal into her mouth before she said, "Grandma."

Pat corrected her. "Pat."

With a mouthful of cereal, Honey said, "Pat, could you not smoke around me? You gonna give me second hand smoke!"

"Little girl, I'm not ready for your mouth. I can smoke around you. I smoked around all my kids and ain't nothing..."

Pat fell silent, for a moment it looked like she was going to cry, but that moment passed quickly. Shay finished her cereal and got up to put her bowl in the sink. Pat gave her a look and she went back and washed it out real quick.

"Pat," Honey said. "you forgot to put the cigarette out. That's how you get cancer and I don't want no cancer. Then I'll be bald-head and you'll have to buy me some wigs."

"Ok, little girl," Pat said as she stubbed out her

cigarette in the ashtray. "I hope you don't act like this all the time. You gonna have to learn to leave Pat alone. There little girl, you satisfied?"

"Thank you, grandma. I mean, Grandma Pat," Honey said smoothly.

"Pat, just Pat."

Honey thought about it for a moment. "Nah, I decided I like Grandma Pat better."

Pat took a sip of her drink as Shay walked past. "Shay, where you goin'?"

"To get me a square. Don't worry, I'm going on the back porch so I won't give the princess here cancer." Shay went to her bedroom and got a cigarette out of her purse. She tossed her purse on the bed spilling out some of the contents, but she left it there and flip-flopped her way back through the kitchen and out onto the back porch. She took her time smoking. When she was done, she flicked the butt out into the alley and went back inside.

Before she could leave the kitchen, Pat stopped her. "Shay, I'm gone need you to keep an eye on this little girl before she drive me crazy. I don't need you running the streets, neither. It's too much going on. Once I bury Nay and Dee, I think we're gonna move. Maybe even out of town. It's about time. That's prolly what we need, a new start. I know you gone miss yo' lil friends, but look at it this way, now they got a place to visit outta town. They ain't gone leave the Chi, no way."

"Ain't nobody been in the streets, Pat," Shay said. "I been in the house tryna to stay out the way. I can't trust nobody,ain't no love. I'm with you on the move. I just don't wanna be here anymore."

Honey finished her bowl of cereal and went to put the bowl in the sink. She turned to Pat. "Grandma Pat, I'm going to get my toys and I'm going to watch the big TV in the front. I want to watch Frozen again. Is that okay?"

Pat waved her hand. "Yeah bih…I mean child, go right on ahead. Anything to keep you from messing with me. Gone 'head, lil girl. Sit down, Shay."

Honey left the kitchen and Shay took a seat at the table across from Pat. Her mother lit her cigarette again. "Shay, I know this is a hard time, but if you need to talk or something I'm always here."

Shay interrupted, "You have got to be kiddin', Pat. Don't get in yo' feelings now! I definitely don't want to talk. Not now. Not after everything that has happened. When I needed to talk way back when, you told me, I better get heartless because ain't no love in this world. That was your answer to everything and so being your child it became mine, too. Don't change now! Don't let it not be the way to be, now. So, no thank you, Pat. I'm good. Talking ain't gone bring back Nay, or Dee, or free Jay."

Pat looked at her like she wanted to say something, but seemed to think better of it. "Well, I guess you learned what I taught you," Pat said.

"Yeah, that's what we'll call it," Shay said as she left her seat. "I'm about to go see what this little girl is doing. She is way too quiet."

In Shay's room, Honey was collecting her dolls so they could watch Frozen with her, when she noticed the contents of Shay's purse spilled onto her bed. Amidst the makeup, weed, and cigarettes and other clutter, there was Shay's gun.

Transfixed, Honey almost levitated to the gun. She picked it up and found out it wasn't heavy at all. She pointed it at her dolls. "Bang, bang, bang," she mouthed.

"Honey!" Shay yelled, startling her niece. Honey swung the gun around when Shay shouted at her, frightening her and pulled the trigger. Bang! Bang! Bang! Shay screamed and fell to the ground. Blood gurgled, and then gushed from a hole in her neck. Several shattered teeth lay on the floor as blood poured out of her mouth.

Pat had just lit another cigarette in the kitchen when she heard the shots. Without leaving her seat at the kitchen table, she hollered, "Shay, what was that noise? Shay? Shay, you and Honey better stop playin' with me! Shay! Shay! You hear me calling you?! Shay!"

What happened to...

Pat – After burying her children, she used the insurance settlement from Nayshawn and Dee's deaths to move to Atlanta and ball out for a while. Though she still prides herself on being heartless, she takes care of her granddaughter Honey and her paraplegic daughter Shay, while she runs the All Heart daycare center.

Shay – Though paralyzed from the waist down, she works at Pat's daycare. She rocks a mouthful of gold, diamond teeth, and keeps her gun on her side. She tells anybody that will listen that she will always rep Chicago.

Plena – Went back to school and got her high school diploma. After graduating she went to Olive Harvey junior college where she took the Fire Department test. She passed the test and she took a job as a Paramedic.

Jayshawn – Was tried as an adult for five murders and 7 attempted murders on a police officer. Months after his 18th birthday, he lost a short trial and was sentenced to 200 + years. His projected parole date is 2245. He still raps in prison and becomes extremely violent if his deceased twin is mentioned negatively.

Cat – Won $5000 a week for the rest of her life from a scratch-off ticket she spent her last five dollars on. When her boyfriend, now her children's father four times over, got off of parole they moved to Florida where they own a boat and several luxury cars.

Trish – Is somewhere getting as high as gas prices.

Que – Never recovered from the mickey pill Dee slipped in his lean. He lived for two years with his mother and grandfather before having a seizure in his sleep, which caused him to die from swallowing his own tongue. He never saw Honey again, if he had, he wouldn't have recognized her.

Treadwell – Turned down the eight years the State offered thinking the charges against him were going to be dropped in return for snitching on the Bangout Twins. When he lost his trial, the judge promptly sentenced him to 768 months as a habitual offender. After being revived because he fainted, Treadwell had to go back to his cell and get a pen and paper to figure out how much time he'd been given.

Cabo – Is still around the hood sending the little homies off daily.

Patron – Never recovered from the mickey pill he swallowed after finding it in the bag of money he took from Dee after murdering her. He spent the rest of his days coloring and drooling in a state mental institution.

Kevo – He used the money from the duffel bag to open a custom car body shop.

Det. Farillo and Williams – Remained partners until Farillo caught COPD from smoking cigarettes and Williams had several heart attacks and was forced to retire.

Discussion <u>Questions</u>

<u>Chapter 1 Discussion Questions</u>

1. If your mother or father talked to you the way Pat talks to Shay would you have a problem with it? How would you let them know without being disrespectful?
2. In your opinion is Shay disrespectful in the way she responds to her mother's questions?
3. Do you think being sexually active at the age of 16 is normal in today's society?
4. Shay is definitely well aware of her sexuality, can she be considered promiscuous?

<u>Chapter 2 Discussion Questions</u>

1. Is it clear that Shay's father's absence plays a big part in her life?
2. Often parents assume things like their drug abuse and neglect don't affect a child when the child is too young to know. Is that true or false?
3. Can it be considered dangerous to approach new situations with a negative attitude?
4. Though she is sexually active, Shay knows very little about sexually transmitted diseases. Is that a problem?
5. Shay doesn't seem to be too concerned that she has an STD, though a minor one. Do you think she will be more careful in the future?

Chapter 3 Discussion Questions

1. What do you think are some of Nayshawn and Jayshawn's influences in life? Music? The street/gang culture? Social media?
2. The twin boys seem so eager to please the older gang members, why do you think that is?
3. The boys easily assume a role in the hood's beef. Is that right or wrong, or just how the hood is?
4. Drugs play a part in poor decision making. True or false?
5. Clearly the older boys used the Twins to do their dirty work, why didn't the Twins see that?
6. Do you think it was love for the hood, peer pressure, clout chasing or just wanting to be accepted that make the Twins murder those innocent people?

Chapter 4 Discussion Questions

1. The studio seems like a place Shay and her friends go to clear their minds, do you have a place like that? A friend's house? The gym? The library?
2. Does music influence the thinking of teens/young adults? If so, how?
3. With 1 being the least and 100 being the most of how mad your parents would be if they knew you were skipping school, what do you think your parents' number would be?
4. Even though Shay has a STD she appears to have

sex with Ace without mentioning it, do you think that happens a lot in real life?

5. Are your close circle of friends more of a negative or positive influence on you? Answer truthfully.

Chapter 5 Discussion Questions

1. Dee is obviously younger than Que, do you think she is in over her head with him?

2. Though she obviously has a good plan for them, why doesn't Que want to listen to her? Is it because of his ego?

3. Does it seem like Que and Dee have a healthy relationship or a dysfunctional one? Why?

4. Have you ever been in a situation where, though you were younger, you were wiser than others around you? Tell us about it.

5. Is she wrong for trying to change Que's spending habits and he's the reason they're able to get the money?

Chapter 6 Discussion Questions

1. Has gun violence affected your life? The life of a friend or loved one?

2. Three children died as a result of the Nayshawn and Jayshawn's actions, do you think families ever fully recover from tragedies like that?

3. Do you believe that some people are just in the wrong place at the wrong time?

4. There can be lots of shootings in a city the size of

Chicago, do you think people get used to it?

5.   Do you believe in coincidences?

Chapter 7 Discussion Questions

1.   Do you think the girls that decided to pick on Cat because they had the upper hand regretted it?

2.   Sometimes the consequences to our actions show up when you least expect it. Tell us about a time that happened to you.

3.   If you ever been jumped on, how did you feel afterwards?

4.   Trish seems to be becoming really untrustworthy, why do you think that is?

Chapter 8 Discussion Questions

1.   Does Treadwell seem like a positive or negative influence on Jayshawn and Nayshawn?

2.   Did Treadwell's explanation of what kind of person Snipes really was make a difference to the Twins?

3.   If you notice a good friend doing something stupid do you let them know? If your answer is yes, give an example.

4.   It seems hard at a young age to tell who is really there for you in life, why is that?

5.   Did Nayshawn make a huge mistake admitting to Treadwell about the murders they'd committed?

Chapter 9 Discussion Questions

1. Did you ever have to deal with rejection? What did you do?
2. Does it seem like Que isn't really speaking his mind?
3. If you're in a relationship do you have a problem with what your significant other does on social media?

Chapter 10 Discussion Questions

1. Do you think Patron got what he deserved for showing a stranger so much of his personal business?
2. Have you ever met someone that you thought you could trust and later found them to be untrustworthy? Are you still friends with that person?
3. Why do you think Shay is able to set someone like Patron up to be robbed with no remorse?

Chapter 11 Discussion Questions

1. In your opinion is Treadwell wrong for telling on Nayshawn and Jayshawn?
2. Do you think he would have told on them if it didn't help him out with his own case?
3. How would you feel knowing you're hanging out with someone that killed three innocent people for no reason?

Chapter 12 Discussion Questions

1. Do you feel like Shay, Swan and Ace are hardened criminals or just troubled children?
2. Often people say, "they're doing what they gotta do to survive", do you feel like that's the truth or an excuse to do certain things?
3. Though the Twins have committed a triple homicide, they still act like regular kids, does that amaze you?
4. Shay is infatuated with Ace though he has a woman he lives with and a child, is she wrong?
5. Is Ace's child's mother wrong for her actions?

Chapter 13 Discussion Questions

1. Social media and what their followers think seems to be a huge priority with Shay and her friends, why do you think that is?
2. Trish steals out of Shay's purse, have you ever had someone you considered a friend steal from you? What did you do about it? If you resorted to violence was it worth it in your opinion?
3. Did you think that Shay would share her newfound wealth with her friends? Why or why not?
4. Is the type of relationship that Ace and Shay have, what people mean when they say their relationship is "complicated"?
5. Swan can be considered opportunistic or thirsty, would you hang around with a friend like him?
6. The things her brothers have been doing come as

a complete shock to Shay, should she be angry or not care at all?

Chapter 14 Discussion Questions

1. Trish puts herself in some pretty dangerous situations chasing a high. Do you agree or disagree?
2. Do you know what are some of the long term effects of drug use? Describe some.
3. Do you know what are some of the long term effects of alcohol on the body? Describe some.
4. Like a lot of people that abuse drugs or alcohol, Trish has a lot of negative things going on in her life. Describe some of the things she's dealing with that might make her want to get high.
5. Are the Twins and their friends morally wrong for taking advantage of Trish?

Chapter 15 Discussion Questions

1. As a pa---rent, Pat never seems to be there for her children, is that a problem?
2. Do you think they make better decisions without her input? Explain.
3. Shay uses social media to expose Swan's disloyalty to Ace and Swan posts a video of her in return, is that fair?

Chapter 16 Discussion Questions

1. Is it wise for Nayshawn and Jayshawn to make rap songs about their crimes?
2. The Twins don't seem to be worried about the police, is that because of their youth and ignorance?
3. Did the Twins overreact to Swan posting footage of their big sister in a compromising position?

Chapter 17 Discussion Questions

1. Pat doesn't seem to have a real problem with Shay doing illegal things, should she?
2. Shay got a kick out of the video Swan posted of her, is that normal?
3. Has someone ever done something negative to you that you spun into a positive thing? Explain.

Chapter 18 Discussion Questions

1. Do you think Ace really had the right to be mad at Swan? After all, Shay is not his girlfriend.
2. Evidently Ace had feelings for Shay, should he just have admitted that to Swan?
3. Is your friendship with your best friend strong enough to get past something like what happened between Ace and Swan?
4. Was it noble for Jayshawn and Nayshawn to defend their sister's honor?
5. Did the Twins go too far?

Chapter 19 Discussion Questions

1. Do you often find it hard to listen to your parent(s) when it comes to relationships with friends?
2. Have your parents ever warned you about someone and at first you couldn't see it, but as time passed you did?
3. Do you think Dee really loves Que or is she sticking around for the money?
4. Have you ever treated someone wrong that didn't deserve it? Did you regret it?
5. Is Dee wrong for seeking revenge for Que's betrayal?

Chapter 20 Discussion Questions

1. Trish seems to be okay, did you think she would be after taking those drugs the night the Twins found her?
2. Wouldn't it have been less trouble for Shay to just forgive Trish and stop being her friend than to try and jump her?
3. There seems to be no shortage of older men/boys trying to take advantage of Shay, is that because of how she carries herself?
4. Does Shay give up on her education too easily? Would you?
5. Things had really spiraled out of control and Shay doesn't feel like she has anyone she can turn to. Who do you turn to when things are bad like they were for her?

Chapter 21 Discussion Questions

1. Nayshawn and Jayshawn don't seem to know that their violent acts have real life consequences. Do you think many teens/young adults think the same way?
2. The Twins illegal drug use has definitely escalated, do you understand why?
3. Violent acts like carjacking affect innocent people, is that fair?
4. The Twins didn't seem to have any positive influences, do you believe that's the reason things end like they did for them?
5. If you lost your brother or sister, do you think you would ever be the same? (If you have actually, can you discuss it?)

Chapter 22 Discussion Questions

1. In your opinion, does Pat love her children?
2. The death of a loved one affects us all differently. Name some ways you've seen people around you affected by losing someone.
3. People like Pat aren't born, they're made. What are some things you think that would make a young mother of four children as heartless as Pat?
4. In her mind, Pat gave her sons everything she could think of to buy, but they still turned out badly. What do you think was missing?

Chapter 23 Discussion Questions

1. Should Dee have just taken Honey and left Que for good?
2. It's said that hurt people, hurt people. Does that apply to this situation?
3. Does Que deserve what happens to him for plotting to betray the mother of his child?
4. Do you believe if money wasn't involved Que and Dee could have worked things out?

Chapter 24 Discussion Questions

1. The tables have turned on Shay, has that ever happened to you?
2. If you needed to get away from your life for a few days, where would you go?
3. Should Ace and Swan's friends be mad at Shay for what the Twins did to them?

Chapter 25 Discussion Questions

1. In your community, do you feel like police hurt more than they help or vice versa?
2. Was Pat's reaction to the policemen normal or abnormal to you?
3. Rarely do some families receive counseling after tragedies like what happened to Nayshawn. Do you think counseling helps heal a family?
4. Would you agree to counseling if you were in a similar situation?

Chapter 26 Discussion Questions

1. The street/gang culture demands that the participants retaliate for any wrongs done to them, so can the fighting/violence ever truly come to an end?
2. Some people find it really easy to take someone's life. How do you feel about that?
3. Dee is killed because of Shay's actions. Do you understand how your actions can affect those around you? Explain.
4. Do you think what happened to Dee was Karma or cause and effect?

Chapter 27 Discussion Questions

1. Do you think the past events will bring Pat and Shay closer?
2. How do you think Pat remains sane after losing three of her children?
3. Pat had children by the wrong kind of men, in your opinion did that affect the way Shay and Dee dealt with males?
4. Do you think Honey has a real chance at a normal life?